## Praise for *The Mango Tree*

"I loved the intimate voices, the speaking landscapes, the gorgeous, heartbreaking world contained in *The Mango Tree*. This is a marvelous read to be returned to again and again."

—Nancy Horan,
author of *Loving Frank*

"*The Mango Tree* is an extraordinary book by an extraordinary man. Fifty years ago, in his debut novel—*The Joshua Tree*—Robert Cabot gave elegiacal expression to the nascent consciousness of the environmental movement. Now, in his centenary year, the world is waking up to what he was among the first to see: the existential threat to life on Earth posed by human plunder and depredation.

Think of Cabot's visionary novels, *The Joshua Tree* and *The Mango Tree* as book-ends to his life's work: giving voice to our home planet. In this valedictory, though he acknowledges humankind's failure to heed his cri de coeur, he does not despair. Rather, as seer and activist, Cabot brings to mind Shelley's dictum—*Poets are the unacknowledged legislators of the world.*"

—Robert Fuller,
physicist, author, social reformer,
citizen diplomat, former president of Oberlin College

"A wonderful novel... beautiful, mysterious, touching."

—Jesús Acosta,
Emeritus teacher, Alamos, Mexico

## Praise for Previous Works

***The Joshua Tree***

"A novel of enormous talent and distinction, lyrical, resonant, evocative, unusual... written *con amore*... tremendous control and skill... a first-rate book."

—William Fadiman

"An achievement for the art of letters... a book that belongs in print for the sake of the world."

—Malcolm Cowley

***That Sweetest Wine***

Robert Cabot's new book is as good a piece of writing as anything coming out of the United States. *That Sweetest Wine* deserves and surely will get wide readership."

—Farley Mowat

***The Isle of Khería***

"In his enchanting, powerful book *The Isle of Kheria* Robert Cabot's passionate connection to the natural world animates gorgeous landscapes in Greece, in Italy and in the American Northwest. This story of a life-long friendship between two men is alive with vibrant details and told in Cabot's extraordinary musical, sonorous, evocative voice."

—Susan Cheever

***Time's Up! A Memoir of the American Century***

"Robert Cabot's elegant and touching memoir of his search for personal meaning and the shaping of a world of compassion and justice. Given the current environmental and geopolitical state of the world, this cri de coeur is sure to resonate deeply."

—Lewis John Carlino,
film director and playwright

# The Mango Tree

ALSO BY ROBERT CABOT

*Time's Up! A Memoir of the American Century*
*The Isle of Kheria*
*That Sweetest Wine: Three Novellas*
*The Joshua Tree*

# The Mango Tree

Robert Cabot

Laughing Diamond
Publishing

Published by Laughing Diamond Publishing LLC
6540 Ebb Tide Lane, Freeland, Washington 98249
Manufactured in the United States of America.

Cover art by Lauraine Ayers-Briel
Interior design by Katharine Prince.
Author photograph © 2023 Kevin Horan.
Typeset in Adobe Garamond Pro.
First edition.
1987654321

This is solely a work of fiction. The names, characters, events, and places are either invented by the author or are being used fictitiously.
Any resemblance to actual people, whether alive or dead, events, or places is entirely coincidental.

ISBN 978-0-929701-98-1 (hardcover : acid-free paper)

*to Penny*

# PART I

Felipe Valenzuela, a name for a Mexican Iguanito? I've told you before, Ramiro son. The tyranny of the Díaz regime. They enslaved us, sold us to hacienda land barons who forced these names on us.

But... here, sit by me. It's time you heard more.

Diaz. His army destroyed our village on the Iguanito River, slaughtered most of us. My parents and I with thirty others were selected to be sold as slaves. I was ten, the youngest, but tall, fit.

Driven south by three soldiers on horses. Endless weeks of horror. Chained with our hands in front so we could eat the rotten bits they'd throw in the dust before us.

Deaths.

My parents fed me whatever they could grab. They protected me from the others so I could get a drink from streams, from rain puddles on the endless roads and trails. They starved. They died together. Their bodies dragged into the cholla. Your grandparents, Miro.

In Oaxaca we were sold to a land baron. Sixty pesos a head. Weeks more staggering south. To an endless timber and henequenda hacienda. To clearing forests, digging irrigation ditches, tending their crops, their animals.

They whipped us regularly, raped our women, tagged us all with one family name, Valenzuela. Yes, Ramiro, there, in the hills of southern Mexico, I became Felipe Valenzuela.

Two years of brutal slavery. Several of us died. I was twelve when we escaped, twenty-three of us.

Slipping away one by one, the guards asleep, to the gathering place by the stream side beyond the first henequén field. We meet under the arching roots of a giant fig tree, watched in the half-moon light by a family of sloths as they slowly unwind from each other, from their nighttime perches in the branches.

When the moon has set, we slip away, crouching, one by one.

Slow marches, the weakest, the smallest leading the way. To straggle hopelessly behind is to die, as three of us have. Months yet to go, a thousand kilometers, more, to our desert homeland.

Our Comandante has a bit of a hollow branch he drums with a stone. Warrior songs, softly, though, voices low, keeping time with the weariest footsteps up ahead. A daytime march on mountain tracks, pine forests, streams, vultures circling overhead. In the valleys we march mostly at night to avoid the roving mercenaries. They'd round us up, drive us back south, sell us again, what's left of us, to the plantation slavers.

There in the valleys, when the jungle is thick and tangled and a light carries nowhere, we do dare to pick our way with pine-pitch torches. Red cat's eyes, the ocelots and pumas and jaguars, waiting, hungry, watching for a straggler.

No one knows more than the general direction that we must go, not even our Comandante. For much of the march, the driving of us down to the plantation fields two years ago, the leaders had been blindfolded. The rest, we were so weakened by hunger, the wounded feet, the regular lashings, that our surroundings were a blur.

We are guided by the sun, the moon, the stars, the moss on tree trunks would be on the sunless northern side. In the thick jungles, when we can see no sky, no sun, no stars, they would send one of us boys up the tallest tree. Some trees are easy, many branches, smooth bark, no thorns. The palm trees are the worst. Bare feet to cling to the hairy branchless trunks, a loop of rope we'd woven from grasses around our waist and the tree trunk, each lurch up or down is a wink at death. And there is the dense growth of fronds at the top. You'd hope to get above the nearby trees, pick out the polar star.

Late one night, in the thickest jungle yet, a huge thunderstorm catches us. Drenched even here under the thick jungle cover, faint with hunger, no protection, no place to hide from approaching daylight. And with no recent look at the stars, we have lost all sense of direction.

In a flash of lightning, just in front of us, a doorway of immense cut slabs of stone. It's wrapped in roots and lianas. In the next flashes we see that we are at the base of a pyramid, giant steps reaching up into the flaming clouds. The open doorway, half hidden behind twisting vines, leads into a crypt, powdery dry. The air is thick with the chirping of bats and the sharp smell of their droppings. Protection from the storm, from the daylight, and a lookout far above the jungle to find our directions the following evening. We hear the bats returning, gorged on night insects. By feel and by luck, in the total darkness, we manage to pull dozens from their toeholds, twist their necks, and find a bit of nourishment, a few drops of blood, a bite or two of stringy raw meat from their scrawny corpses.

When we must cross a grassy plain, no cover, no way around, we wait for the moon to set, wipe black mud on the hands and faces of those cursed with lighter skin, run quickly through the pampas, stooped and silent but for the squawk of a bird we'd kicked from sleep.

I am twelve, I am strong, I march at the very end. Our Comandante puts me there. Allow no stragglers, my son. The next day Comandante Mateo and Cristina ask me to be their son.

My sadness, my gladness.

I dream of a day when I shall dance the Iguana, my mask so ugly, dance with Coyote in his headdress, dance till he drops from exhaustion. I dance on, dance there in the firelight in our rebuilt village, dance with the Iguanitos circling, with the drum-drumming and the fiddling through the night.

~

Yes, Ramiro, we rebuilt the village. Others joined, lone families begging for help. We recaptured roaming horses, celebrated a wondrous first harvest. Our river was full of fish.

We were aware of dangers, of Díaz's army, of roaming bands. We kept guards out day and night. But there were no sightings, no alarms. Then, on my fifteenth birthday . . .

The clatter of my heart, tap-tapping. My rattling teeth. Can they hear, will they find me too, burn me to a cinder with the rest of the village? I know what they do, these soldiers. Me, Felipe, crouched with the scorpions and the gilas, a finger of the sun pointing straight at me through a hole in the tin roof, will they drag me out with the others, slash through my ribs, tear out my heart to see why it hammers so?

Have they gone now? Their boots stamping in the dust, the shouts, the commands, the slam of machetes on flesh and bone, the gush and splatter just outside this crumble of adobe. It is quiet now, only a whimper, a sob, a dog howling somewhere up the street. Do I dare? Careful, it's dark in here, tools and cans and clattery things, careful. Look out through this crack where the mud and straw have melted away.

A head hangs by his long white hair from the dead branch of a lime tree, his genitals in his mouth, blood drip-dripping in the dust. His body is stripped naked, propped against the belly of his beheaded stallion. I shiver in clammy sweat, my stomach heaves vomit, I curl trembling into the dark. The dog again, her wail lingers in the crackle of flames, in this bitter smoke—my village that is no more.

I watch the finger of sun move slowly down my left arm, onto my thigh, my knee, yellow on black skin, burning through splotches of dust. Burning on my shin, deep to the bone, a drop of blood crusting, a curl of smoke, the sweet stink of burning flesh. Will it burn through the bone, cut my leg clean, seal the bleeding? No pain, no tears. Silence screaming in the dark? That dog, she come closer, scratching in the ashes, a whimper. I'll crack open the door, throw out a headless chicken for her to gnaw.

I creep through the dust, hands and knees, push at the door, it creaks like a woman birthing, rayos! I peer out into the sunlight. The bitch, she slinks by, deaf to the rusty screech, ignoring my stench. Yellow, dugs dragging, tail tight between her legs, she sniffs at the raw flesh of the stallion's severed head. She backs off, bares her teeth in a wary snarl, shuffles away. I crawl half out the door. Only the spitting of the flames where the thatch was still green, only a beaten bitch. Beyond the end of our single street, our stone church stands against the afternoon sun. There are flames in the steeple's openings, the beams are burning. A sound of splitting, a crash, a single clang. Our bell is dead.

Careful, crouched, I step out, empty, ash dry. Dust sticks to my left foot, a pad of dust. My ankle wobbles. Behind me is a black puddle of his blood with a footprint.

My stomach rolls upside down. I scrape and scrape on a paloverde stump, hopping on the other foot. The bitch sees me, turns, comes toward me, almost sidewise, a crab on the river shingle, one yellow eye looking up at me. We'd kick her, her whining and begging, we would... No, she licks my leg, I kneel, hold her, my tears spot her dusty hide.

She follows me as I steal in the shadows of the banana trees where the smoke is thickest, stooping like Bisabuela did for years before she died. Scared, but there is no one, no sound but the dying fires, the squealing of a flock of little parrots. No one. My Mamaíta, Papaíto, a childless couple, now me. They had gone at daybreak to the sesame field to tie up the sheaves. I'd creep there, carefully, maybe find them, maybe.

She touches my knee, whines, we stop. Hanging from the branch of a mesquite, hanging from one foot tied with leather thongs around the ankle, naked, their sex bloody, running red still down one side and dripping off their fingers, a man and a young girl. I cannot look in their faces, I must not know them. I hide behind my hands, cower, turn away. Choking, whimpering, we, the two of us, creep on.

The village fields are not far. I duck low out among the sheaves, but there is no place there for them to hide. I crouch behind a thicket of prickly pear. Likely hiding places, where they might still be? On the edge of the field there was an abandoned wellhole where I had often played. It was mostly filled with stones cleaned from the fields, and was grown over with a tangle of weeds. I make my way to it without stepping again into the open. They are there, Mamaíta and Papaíto. Whispers, a finger to the lips, they beckon to me. I jump down, we cling together. Perrita jumps down too, licks at our tears. They make me drink the last bit of water from the gourd Papaíto has on a thong about his neck. I chew on a shred of salted fish from their lunch bag.

We wait for the dark, for the last sad song from a white-winged dove, for the blood-red sky to die. We start off.

An evening breeze from the sea carries our village smoke with us through the night. By dawn there are eleven of us. One by one, shadows in the starlight join us. Five men, one woman, two boys, a small girl. The men know the secret trails through the thorn forests, on to the mountains far to the east where escape is possible.

We stop from time to time to rest, to talk quietly of the horrors, to get some idea from new arrivals, of who may have survived. To wait in the hopes that others would slip through the night to join us. Most of the village women had been caught in their homes, raped, beheaded. The men had been in the fields, they are all still carrying their machetes, ready in their hands or tied to their waists.

During the day we hide in a cave in the bank of an arroyo. The men had caught three rabbits in the early morning, chopping them as they came out of their warrens. We chew the raw flesh, not daring to start a fire, suck water from cactus pulp. In the dusk, as we are getting ready to set out again, we hear the shuffle of footsteps. A soldier passes close to the mouth of our cave, dragging his feet, exhausted, lost, his rifle trailing in the dust. Rifugio leaps out behind him, kicks the rifle out of his hand, grabs him with his forearm around his neck, throws him to the ground. He struggles to his knees, pleading that he was lost, that he too is Indio Bravo, that he wants to join us.

Vete a la mierda, guey! Chinga tu madre!

The soldier prays for the love of merciful Nuestra Señora, holding his hands before him palm to palm. On a wrist is a wide horsehair bracelet.

My wife's bracelet, pinche! And with blows of his machete Rifugio cuts off both feet.

While they hold him and tie his hands behind him with his belt, writhing, shrieking till they stuff a stone in his mouth. Refugio wipes the blood and sand off his machete on a bit of grass, picks up the severed feet, takes off the boots, throws the feet to Perrita, ties the boots together with their laces, and slings them around his neck. Better than barefoot when his huaraches wear out. Papaíto goes through the soldier's pockets and kit. A handful of coins, a half a bottle of pulque, a canteen of water, three moldy tortillas, a bit of meat jerky wrapped in a filthy bandana. He hands these to Mamaíta. He picks up the rifle, slings two full bandoliers over his head and shoulder. With a finger to his lips, he beckons to us all to go. We set off quickly up the arroyo. A slice of a moon is stuck on the thorns of an etcho above us, the crimson sky darkening over the sea far behind.

We move on in the moonlight, in the shadows of the mesquite, Refugio ahead of me, boots swinging from his shoulder. We'd left the soldier gagging, teeth rasping on stone, life puddling out, black into the dust. My teeth chatter, I whimper, I cannot help it, I cannot stop. Mamaíta touches my cheek, her thumb rough to my tears. Perrita, she's always at my side now, reaches up, her front paws up on my leg, she licks my hand.

The moon slides down behind us, red, scratched by the thorns of the ocotillo, slides into the far sea. Darkness closes in. Feeling our way now, holding to each other, a hand or belt or a sarape. Mamaíta, behind me, holds onto my shirt. I reach out, touch a dangling boot, sticky. I pull back in horror, I wipe my fingers violently on my thigh, reach again, find the tip of Papíto's long braided hair.

Far ahead the sky grays ever so slightly, mountain teeth cut into the dawn. Birds begin their chatter, a dove mourns. On a kapok branch above me an owl stretches his wings against the last faint star, hoots his evil call, settles into sleep. A coyote yips from across the ravine. A doe calls softly to guide her yearling, to guide us. The chirp of an iguana to encourage us. We are silent, Perrita too, she's learned silence to survive. No whispers, no wails for loss, only my whimper and the cry of a frightened fawn.

We can see enough now to let go of each other, to move faster up the dry stream bed. Papaíto stops, points to a cave in a low rock wall dimly lit above us. We clamber up, a jaguar's home, its animal smell sharp and dangerous. It's deep enough for all of us. The floor is littered with bones and bits of fur pelts. There is a cleared area in the back, the dust smoothed, where the jaguar family slept, Mamaíta says. Refugio takes first watch, lying back of the cave's lip, machete ready if Jaguar would return. Or soldiers, driven through the night by rage and lust and reward. Gold coins for a scalp, or a nose, silver for two ears. Yes, even the little children know this.

Six children. Four of us are with our parents, two sisters are alone. They had whispered, through their tears and sobs, to my Mamaíta, and I heard them, back there hiding in the old well hole. They were playing in a patch of cane when they saw soldiers pull their mother and their father from the roof they were thatching, hack them into pieces, tie their scalps to their belts. The sisters cling together now in the jaguar stink, keeping apart from us. They won't say anything to us, they won't look at us.

Why are they ashamed, Mamaíta?

I am so hungry, thirsty, but the gourds are empty, the rabbits stay safe in their warrens, and we dare not use the rifle we took from the soldier. An iguana, fat and dusty, blinks at us with a red eye. No, we are of his People, we would not eat him, no, never.

The sun is fire when I peek out, they hiss me back out of sight, angry. I sleep.

Thin sleep, dream's edge, a bat hangs just over my head. Out through the toothless mouth of the cave I see the shadows lengthen, the colors begin to fade. We are stirring, sitting up, readying for our night's march. On watch now, Emilio raises a hand of warning, gestures back at us for silence. Faintly we can hear the clatter of a stone in the creek bed, a tearing and munching. Word comes back that there are two mules just below us. They are hobbled, there is no one in sight. Papá and Emilio are whispering. They tell us they will scout the surroundings, for a white man's ranch must be nearby.

They return, no one. We sneak down in the dusk. The men take the mules, a mula and a macho, by their forelocks. They untie the hobble ropes from the fetlocks, tie them around the mules' noses and necks like halters, something to hold onto, lead them. They seem docile, well fed, much better than the few we'd had in our village. The three youngest children are put onto the mula, dock to withers in order of size, hanging on to the mane and neck and to each other. We other three will walk. Concepción is to ride the macho. Her husband and daughter were the ones hanging by one ankle from that village tree. Her belly sticks far out, lifting her filthy white skirt above her knees muy embarazada. She waddles over, hands to the small of her back to ease the weight. They hoist her onto the macho. Her seat is unsteady, she cannot lean forward onto the withers with her arms around the mule's neck, her belly with child is so very big. A tight hold on the mane will have to do. Her head bends down, chin to her breast, she is sobbing softly.

Papaíto in the lead, we move out. Emilio to guard our rear, staying well back. I hear them tell him to keep off to the side of the rocky arroyo bed, silent in the soft earth, balls of his feet first, feel for dead branches and leaves that would snap or crunch, and stay ready with your machete for any pursuit, soldiers, a rancher. But we'd all know that, why do they bother to say it to him?

Another march, another escape, will the white men always be at our heels? Can they never let us be? Can we somehow throw them back into the sea, or conquer them into slavery?

Mamaíta, you look so tired. Here, my hand, I'll help you along. And maybe sometimes you'll want to hold on to the macho's tail. We'll stay just behind him, maybe help Tia Concepción too, talk to her, keep her awake. Vale Mamá?

The dark has settled in around us, the sky draining from grays to an immense black dome lit golden as the stars and the milky veil of the Via Lactea find their places. Sometimes, when the banks rise and forms dim, we have to hold onto each other. Mostly, though, we manage better than last night. Maybe an hour has gone by when the bestias become edgy, excited. They whinny and the men grab at their noses to make them stop. Stubborn, they pull hard toward a sort of niche in the far bank. Water! And we keep them from it, all their slobbering and pawing and muddying, until the children and Concepción can be lifted off and we all drink and fill the gourds. Emilio slips up, reassures us, drinks, and is gone again. Then it's the turn of the bestias. Their sucking and blowing and the splatter of their pissing. The riders are lifted up, and we move on quickly, extra quiet.

We've come onto a stretch where the trail is no more than a narrow shelf high on the face of the cliff. A half-moon lights our way. Clumps of mescalito air-eaters cling on the rock faces, tufts of grass survive in dusty cracks on the very edge where travelers' feet would not tread. Macho, just ahead of Mamaíta, Papaíta's hand on his halter. Macho stops. He pulls free, stretches down for a bite. Hey! None of that! Macho tearing at a tuft of grass. Concepción, sobbing quietly, slumps over her belly. Bareback, she slides down Macho's neck, over his head. In the wings of her skirt, she is gone. A pale ghost floating into the welcoming void, silent but for the fading sigh of the wind in her dress.

Time stops, breath stops. Forever later, the faintest thud echoes in the black cliff faces.

Mamaíta gasps, sinks to her knees, her hands to her face, whispering a prayer. Papaíto beckons us, we must move on, quickly. In a few paces we come to a gully in the rock face. We turn up. Around a bend it opens out into a small level area, hidden, surrounded by rock walls. Dry grasses, two low junipers, and a trickle of water.

We shall stop here for the day, it will be light soon. Four of us will go back and down into the gorge, find a cave for Concepción and her child. Yes, you may come too. The others must stay here, rest, post guard at the bend in the gully. You may find some roots or berries, and watch for a rabbit, a bird perhaps, snakes, lizards, even iguanas. We must eat.

My Mamá is trembling, her face, though, is fixed, hard like the rock. She drops to the ground, throws herself on her back, arms stretched out, shaking violently. Her eyes unblinking, she stares into the colorless predawn sky.

You must ride the macho tonight, querida.

We, the five of us, head back that evil path looking for a place where we can get down to the ravine bed. At the spot where we lost Concepción, Papá looks carefully at the rock formation behind us, points up to a large black crack in the rock face reaching to the top. He asks us all to remember it as a marker of where to look for the body. We move on. With daylight almost here, one of the men scouts ahead.

In the end, we are forced to go back to where we had started our climb two hours before. We double back into the gorge. The going is difficult, great boulders worn smooth, jagged slabs from the cliffs, high steps of raintime waterfalls. Arrived below the black marker, clear in the morning sun, we separate to look for her in the jumble of rocks. Scrambling about in the area assigned to me, I see a dark splotch near the top of a huge bolder, a sheen of red. Over here! Here!

We find her on the far side of the boulder, wedged in the rocks. We have no carry pole, no blanket to wrap her in, none of her personal things to bury with her. But we do find a small cave above the waterline of summer floods. We carry her up to it. I try not to see her battered face, her naked belly. The men lay her carefully at the back of the cave. One of the men tries for a moment to scratch a cross in the rock above her body but he makes only a faint wavering mark, and my Papá gestures to him to stop. I find a small amapa, no more than a bush leaning out from a shelf in the cliff face, a pocket of earth, just above the flood line. It is in winter flower, a few bluish-pink blossoms. I twist off two bits, bring them to the men. They lay one on her breast for her soul, one on her belly for the soul of the child. That is all, but she will know, the two of them will know, that we have done our best, that they need not play tricks on us in their afterlife, torment us. We have done our best.

We bring rocks to seal the mouth of the cave, pat in mud we scoop from a moist pothole in the stream bed. We climb down, turn to look up at the walled-in cave. We sing a few bits of an ancient song, a few steps of the Death Dance.

Our dead, they will be at peace now. Four fiestas for them, we must not forget.

Yes, I, Ramiro Valenzuela. Son of Felipe and Emerald who are left forever in the desert. Son now of Comandante Jésus and Cristina. Here, this abandoned, crumbling, once wealthy home, one of a rambling line of adjoining houses, stables, courtyards, overgrown gardens, an abandoned shop, an almost empty elementary school.

All joined by an arched covered sidewalk built high to defend against the flooding rains from our mountains. Two–three steps above a cobbled avenue leading from the church to the graveyard. Remnants of a flourishing silver-mining town. A few hundred ranchers, farmers left, and a refuge for surviving Iguanitos.

I am called Miro. I'm a friend of old Donna Raquel. Dear Ragbag, tottery, alone in the home next to ours. A tiny courtyard, one enormous mango tree, a donkey. The town's. She is my friend.

She takes so long, her sticks poking in the dust, her slippers black from the cinders of her mesquite fires for boiling the fruit pastes. I'll help her sell them at Sunday market in the arroyo. Shuffling, pausing, a gasp of sweet air. She brushes a leaf from her hair, gray-white like Abuela's mop. Will she forget to close the outhouse curtain? She'd see me, she'd tell on me, and I'd get boxed about and no more mangoes, the sweetest, juiciest ones in all our town. Do hurry, dear old Ragbag, or the coatis will get there first. No, no, leave your burro be, he's got his bucket and you fed him already when Jesús had unloaded your firewood there against the wall.

I watched from my peeping place as they rolled Donna Raquel onto a board and carried her off.

I see her sleeping in her box, the church bell ringing slowly, calling. Everyone in black, the Sacerdote so solemn. They carry her out on their shoulders, almost drop her when Ruben trips on the new cobbles. No more dust and ruts and summer mud. With the coffin then in a pickup truck and a band in another pickup. Past the grand houses, mostly ruins. A crowd of us, half the town, following, most in our Sunday best. The band plays a lively ranchero they say she'd danced to on her Saint's Day.

On over the arroyo to the Panteón where they put her in the ground. I bring her a twig of her flowering mango. Thank you, old Ragbag, did you know all along that I was sneaking fruit? Is that what you whispered to me, you lying there on your mattress in Mango Tree's shade, wheezing, choking, dying?

~

Now, her home abandoned, I come often. Not when the black clouds come in from the east. The lightning would like to find my Mango Tree, and the thunder that splits my skull, and the rains that fill the arroyos, and the streets that are rivers for hours. I come here with my school work, or a bit of cane to carve into a whistle, or my ball of thread to be beeswaxed for my cobbler Papá, or just me with my no-one-knows thoughts. I sit here in the dust, I lean against my tree, I listen to the white-winged dove lamenting her love betrayed, they say. Soft sobbing, the rustle of feathers, a yellow leaf drops on my knee.

A branch, the lowest, just out of my reach, stretches over me, thick with leaves, with thousands of clustered blossoms, humming with yellow-barred hoverflies. I see her there now, singing softly to herself, my lonely dove. She seems to draw light upon herself, ever so faintly, as if a bit of the sunny cloud that drifts over us has descended, cloaking her, comforting her, a silvery oval of soft light.

The dove's form fades, the oval of light rises, upright, growing, brilliant. A new form appears, held in that glow, filmy, vague, then brighter. It is a woman, all in a dazzling white light. I see her clearly now, every detail. Her gown a wash of crimson, long, buttoned high around her neck, the sleeves loose at her wrists with fringes of gold, it billows about her feet, a cloud of pink floating her ever so lightly. From her head and shoulders she wears a cloak of leaf-green falling to her feet, mingling with the cushioning cloud. Her cloak is sprinkled with yellow blossoms, with flickering stars.

She wears a golden crown.

She smiles down at me, she leans forward, her hands reaching toward me, palms out as if to send something to me. She raises a hand then, a slight gesture. A warm farewell, she fades and is gone, her shining cloud is wisps, vapors lost in the mango blossoms. Even the song is stilled, my lovely dove is gone.

There's a rustling beside me, but I stare on at the empty branch, I brush a tear with the back of my wrist. The rustle again, impatient, I look down. My dove is here beside me, a pink eye calling for attention. She turns to the earth between two shoulders of the mango's roots, begins a flurry of digging. Her claws, her beak, even her wings seem busy sweeping the dust aside. Her head, her breast, her wings are soon covered with bits of leaf, earth, bark, moss. She stops, looks up at me in that sidelong way, hops away, two hops. She watches me for a moment, shakes her head, peeved, hops back to her flurry of digging.

Three times she does this, ever more irritated. She's dug down now perhaps a handspan, and finally I think I understand. I find a bit of stick and start digging. She flies up to the branch, returns to her Evensong. And just then the Vespers bell calls out over our town. Ventura's turn today, swinging on the greasy bell rope with Father beside him looking sweet and holy, his willow switch ready cocked.

I dig on. It is easy, the earth is loose, not at all packed, and in only another handbreadth or two my stick hits something. And there, tipping up out of the dry earth, standing quite by itself against the side of the hole we had dug, spotless. Glistening, though I touched it, just that one poke with my stick, a silver spoon. Maybe a hundred years buried here, maybe? Buried in the times when, with the silver mine quarrels, the violence, many treasures were buried in our town. Maybe a hundred years, yet it is glittering, polished, not a tarnish, not a scratch. A miracle for Ramiro.

Carefully I pick it up, cool from the earth. Small, maybe the length of Abuela's honey spoon. No shorter, no more than the length of my index finger. Carved all over, delicate but worn. An iguana, her tail curled around the bowl of the spoon, her toes tucked in, her tongue a loop at the tip of the handle. On her belly there are faint letters, tiny. In a ray of sunlight I can just make it out. Mi Hijo, my son.

Just then, a large coati, an adventuresome male, leaps from the kapok to my mango, startling the dove from her song. She flies off in a puff of feathers. His tail waving from side to side for balance, he crawls out on a too thin branch, snatches at a lizard, misses, the branch tips down, he falls almost at my feet. He looks at me startled. I jerk my legs in, clutch my spoon to me. Coatis are mean, they can kill our dogs and cats. He is most upset. He jumps up and down three times, bares his teeth at the lizard laughing down at him from the swaying branch. He chirp-chirps angrily, scampers up a vine, out on a branch, over the wall. Gone.

My wondrous silver spoon, my miracle. I hold it to my lips, press it to my heart, warm now, ever so smooth.

From my Lady of the Dove. I'll slice a thong from the fawn skin Papaíto uses for baby shoes, he'll not notice, hang it by its tongue around my neck, hidden under my shirt. They have their crosses of gold, I shall have my silver iguana, my secret.

A crackling, a rustling, leaves in a stray afternoon breeze. My cheek is sore, propped like this on Mango's root shoulder, on the lichens and scraggly mosses. I turn my head. Better. Quite by themselves, my eyes open. I rub them with the back of my wrist. My cheeks are wet, there are dark spots in the yellow dust. Me, Ramiro, returning from dreams, leaving my first parents in the care of the trailside cholla, my mother with that silver iguana spoon about her neck.

Tap-tapping, drifting back, tap-tapping, a woodpecker on that stump of a dead branch. My hand cramps, holding ever so tightly to my shining Iguanito. My dove is back on her branch, quiet now, her belly stuffed with seeds and papaya and the crumbs I'd spread for her, beakfulls of water tipped down her throat from Donna Raquel's abandoned metate. I keep it filled from my school-lunch water bottle.

A piss now, here, on the back side of the mango, makes juicier fruit in the summer, of course. I'll curl up again in the dust, rest my head on a clump of moss. My dove stirs, she shakes a wing, she sleeps.

Iguanita. My grandmother, her friends, even my Comandante second father, they still call my Abuela their

Iguanita. Was it her darkest skin, her pointed nose, her sharpest tongue, her warts and darting ways? No, she says it's from the time when, as a little girl still living in their desert village, the village that is no more, the time when she had a pet iguana. At first he lived in her pocket, but as he grew older, she had him on a leash. Wherever she went, even to the village school, he was always with her. He grew as long as she was tall. Iguanita. And too, she would say, even far beyond the reach of their shaman's memory, the villagers had sometimes called themselves the Iguanitos. At their village fiesta they would tell the story, and dance it to the over-and-over scratchy notes of a fiddle, the thump-thumping of the drums, the story of how the iguana became so ugly.

He'd been beautiful, gentle, always smiling, but the village suffered from the Coyote's tricks, his thieveries and killings. So the gods made the lovely Iguana into the ugliest of all creatures to help the villagers scare away the devil Coyote. A special honor, they said, though he'd had no choice, and I wonder... Well, that's the way of the gods, they say.

The summer sun has climbed down from the branches now, the mango leaves whisper secrets to a fading sky. That dream again, or maybe not a dream, maybe a remembering in my sleep. Will it never leave me be? It was like that, just like that, they say.

A woodpecker tap-taps, tap-taps. Drifting, drifting. Iguanitos, the drum-drumming, their marching song, my Papá, he'd show them the way.

Flaming sky, fading to pale greens, to purples, to stars that dance in my leaves. Birds stir in my branches, settle into sleep, my iguana tick-ticking as she licks up a stream of ants. In this darkness. I, Mango Tree, here I stand.

Three hundred years, three hundred layers of my flesh. No more than a twig when I came, carried from the shadows of white-topped mountains, from the sighs of the sitar, carried in a jar that tasted of honey and spices, carried for many moons. The swaying, the burning of salty spray, the gentle washing. Rich earth, sweet water, shelter. Growing. The dust, the violent tossing. The quiet, cool, lifted from my jar, warm earth, relief, where my roots would stretch out, burrow deep.

Growing, but alone, the only mango tree, a stranger. Friends, yes, my kapok here, others, palms, the etcho cactus, limes, agaves. But I had no brothers. Much later, children would spring from my seed, but not till I was reaching high over the mesquite did I know from scents of the pollen, that others, cousins, had come.

Yes, here I stand, a forest of family and friends about me in the soft night. From the gathering darkness comes a dust-red moon, ragged on one edge. She is held in the arms of the kapok tree, in its tufts of cottony seed. She lifts free, she floats over me, silver now, whispering to me, calling me into her spell. A teasing, drawing up through me from the tips of my roots reaching in the moist earth, suckling. The cool tides rise in me, replenishing, up into my limbs, my leaves, my panicles of tiny yellow flowers. Mother moon, I am grateful to you, your gentle pull. My blossoms that fill with nectar and pollen for the hover-flies, their dusting from flower to flower. That I may bear fruit, sweetened in the sun, sweet for the creatures who will carry my seed.

My creatures.

The winged ones that hang by their toes from a shady branch, sleeping, waiting for the dark to fly off with a bite of golden fruit. The furry ones, their chattering, their singing, their silence. Most have gone now, walled out behind adobe blocks, these white walls of flowering vines. But some still leap to me from my kapok friend, pluck a fruit, always the best, full blushing ones, jump three-legged to a vine, scramble off, nibbling from one paw as they go.

And there are ever more of the mostly hairless two-leggeds, those who cannot fly or leap, who cover themselves with flapping colors, carry off my fruit in baskets. One special one, small, brown, sometimes with no covers. He knows the secret of the garden gate. Cautious, he looks in, waiting for this shuffling-one-with-her-two-sticks to disappear behind her canvas curtain, her place of grunts and groans. Quick now, friend, over there where I'd have dropped some special ones for you. Into your sack with them. Be off with you.

Los Etchos, town of the cactus trees, there's only one in the plaza, and some night someone is angry enough to chop it down too. There are, it's true, plenty of others in the town—street corners, patios—and on the mountainsides among the amapas and mesquites. Shooting baskets in the plaza after school yesterday. A loop of rebar we'd lashed to a cottonwood. I missed six times and got red angry and kicked the ball hard and it crashed into that etcho, Pffftt!

All squished, my ball does make a good pillow now, just fits my head. Lying here in the arroyo dust, still warm from yesterday, lying under a giant etcho, waiting for the dawn light, so I can see the bats. They're here now, come up from their winter in the south. I must see them, see them sucking nectar from the etcho's flowers. White blossoms with their purple petals underneath, they'll close with the sun, later in the day, tight and shriveled. Shiny white on the tips of Etcho's arms, still open as gray light behind the cockscomb of mountains to the east rises into the sky.

There! Two bats, hovering, flower to flower, nibbling, sucking up the nectar, like giant humming birds, tender, wings fanning the petals, tiny squeaks of joy. And they're gone, spiraling into the sun, joining a cloud of others, off, perhaps, to a niche in the cliff there above Abuelo's tannery, to hang by their toes, sleepy from their feasting, rest up, ready to move on with the spring flowerings, on to the north. That's what Abuelo says.

Abuelo says that there are some of us Iguanitos who'd escaped into the hills and forests generations ago, who still use the etchos' bristly brown fruit to comb their hair. When the fruit forms and dries and the bristles stiffen, I'll remember, I'll try that too. And they cook new branches of the etcho, make a magic potion, visit magic places, spirits, the dead.

I'd best go. Though it's Sunday, by now people will begin to be up and about. I'd not want to be found like this. They'd snigger and the whole town would know. Miro, he's gone quite loco.

Adios, old Etcho friend.

Hola Miro, El Negro Flaco! That's what those mestizos boys yell. So? I am tall, skinny, I'm proud of my dark Iguanito skin. Black, the bottom side of a dried mushroom, eyes and hair the color of a bad-luck cat that had just licked off the dust. Hands like a girl's. And that pointy nose.

I'm off to church with Mamá, the bell bong-bonging. Iguana, Coyote, Deer? They do still linger, dance to the drum and the fiddle, but in the barrios, in distant villages, not here in the shadow of the cross. One trinity replaced by another. Dust, a crushing sun, or really by a holy host, what with angels and saints and a multitude of Virgin Marys vying for a privileged place. Father Ignacio, his voice as powerful as ever, though he's in need of an acolyte's help with the altar steps. He had addressed the various dilemmas over the decades by giving only God, his God, the true primacy, and equally for all. True, those of the palest skin still sit in the front rows, we are toward the back, but all are subject to His all-seeing gaze. God keeps the final accounts in Father Ignacio's church. If there are distinctions in those accounts, seeming injustices, that is God's will, a will that must never ever be questioned. Suffering is payment for man's sins, payment He may choose to exact without regard for individual innocence. For Ignacio's God, the individual must be subsumed into the collective. Amen.

So. I, Ramiro, kneeling at the rail, eyes closed, savoring the moment. Murmured blessings, the musty smell of Father's vestments, sweet breath of the censer. Vapors of the wine rising in my head, my wafer slowly melting on my tongue. Ramiro received into the arms of his Lord.

I, Miro, thirteen, batting practice, line drives across the arroyo. Watch out for the nopal, lost a ball there yesterday. I'm good, very good, best averages on the team.

Two months ago: We've decided, Miro, we'll have you on the team, center field, maybe pitch too. But don't come all stinking of rotting cow skin, and leave your crowd of cackling friends where they belong. That's Ricardo, team captain, the mayor's son. White as fresh cheese, brown hair, blue eyes. Six ranches they've bought up, and the town's slaughter shed, and the hides are sold to Abuelo's little tannery.

A few days later, maybe a week, I am walking through the portico on the north side of the plaza, on my way to get our mule, hitch it to the wagon for a load of shoes and saddles and chaparreras to deliver to a buyer in another town, hours away it will be, even at a trot downhill. Ricardo and his crowd have spotted me.

They hold their noses, El Negro Zorrillo, the Skunk-Shitter! I charge at them, out into the plaza where they sprawl on the bandstand steps. I don't get far. The town policeman has been watching, yells, grabs me, drags me back into the portico. Chilito! Out of there! Stay where you belong, pendejo nigger! He wipes his sweaty brown face with a filthy bandana, waves it at the bandstand boys, salutes them with a raucous fart. They cheer, Olé! I escape a thrashing, dive into the tunnels that lace together the old center of Los Etchos. Defenses in the wars, hideouts, trysting, escaping.

Ramiro at the shriving, confessing sinful thoughts. Absolved, he poses bitter questions. God's will, my son, God's will.

A day of batting practice, Ramiro lines a couple to left field, but mostly he's pitching. Home in the half-light, his shoulder painful. He spoons up his sopa de queso with his left hand, but Mamá, she sees him.

I see, I knew you would, pitching all day, you try too hard and you'll never win them over, the Ricardos of our town, pink-white mestizos. We Iguanitos, proud. I brewed this marijuana lotion for you. Here, Ramiro, take off your shirt.

We saddle up the mules, Papá and I, bags tied over the flanks. Dried venison, corn flour, a cook pot, salt, coffee, matches, blankets, hobble ropes, a handful of cartridges, all that's left of them in the coffee can we hide in the cook shed. Rifles slung to the saddle on the offside withers.

Into the higher mountains, hour after hour, avoiding the main trail in the hopes of more likely sighting game. Splashing up shallow river beds, working their way through the chaparral, deeper into the dry deciduous forests, up into the pines, the mists caught in the mountain peaks. No game, nothing but a river otter that ducked into a pool before we could get out our rifles. We camp in an abandoned ranch house, no more than a one-room shed, a collapsing cook house a few steps away, rotting fences. With a hiss and a yowl, a feral cat leaps from the ravaged innards of a stove rusting in the yard, races up a cottonwood, glares down at them, green eyes in the dusk. Papá kicks at the stove. A click of his tongue, a turn of his head, a long blink.

Outsiders. This is the kind of thing that broke them. We'd never bother with a stove up here. Rocks and mud and an iron grill is all you need. More is trouble. Palancas, that's what we called the family, always the beaten look, leaning forward like a wagon brake lever. Sad little family, gone.

Weary, night's upon us, we'll not bother with a fire. Munch a bit of venison jerky, roll into our blankets. Count stars, sleep.

Early morning, still dark, very cold, there's a skin of ice on the water in their cook pot. Papá whispers. Must be quiet, rifles ready. Ramiro, you get a fire going, out of sight, though, there, in the dilapidated cook shed. Boil up the water, a handful of coffee, rifle nearby, keep an eye out back there. Their curiosity may get the better of them, sneak up to see what's going on. Deer are that way. I'll move over nearer the river, get behind a thicket to watch for game at the watering place.

Maybe that iron stove never made it to here, was never used here in the cook shed. Their mud brick stove, the grill crusted with lumps of charred blood and fat, fallen into the ashes, seems still usable. A pile of firewood thick with dust and droppings. A few twigs, break up a branch, one match from the saddle bag, and the fire flames up around the pot.

Some of the wattling on the top half of the shed's back wall has fallen away from the amapa posts, I can see up into the etchos on the hillside, while my fire should be hidden enough from any game that might be looking us over. I have my rifle beside me on this log. They'd axed it flat into a bench. My rifle, old, the stock charred on the butt where maybe someone used it to poke at a fire, cabrón! I've only fired it a few times. Papá gave it to me just last month on my saint's day, and ammo is dear.

I'll have a look out back, pretend I see something. Unclick the safety, there, poke it through this gap in the wattling, rest the barrel, slippery, smells of oil, rest it against this post, propped on this branch stub. Tight against my shoulder so the recoil won't bash me, tight against my cheek, finger ready to squeeze ever so slowly on the trigger. Take aim over the sight notch, aim at that green kapok fruit only a few yards away.

But it disappears, did it just drop from the tree? Something dark, did a hawk light on a branch in front of it, stretch its wings in the morning sun? I shift my aim a hair, just below where my target had been. An enormous ear, it twists back and forth over my sights, in front of my target. Antlers, twin forks, a mule deer buck, as big as, bigger than the one Papá brought in last autumn. I freeze, everything stops, my heart, my breath, the flames under the grate, the smoke, that ever-seeking ear. Can I kill? Yes yes, of course, I must. My head is a rush of red, my finger squeezes slowly, my sights just below that ear. His eye blinks, my gun explodes. He shrieks, leaps straight up, turns quite around in mid air, lands on all four feet. He lowers on his haunches for the next leap, and collapses.

My hands are shaking, my heart is a clamor, a hammering in my head. Carefully, gently I put the rifle down in its place on the log bench. I stand in the dilapidated gloom, cut by a knife edge of sun through the wattling.

My boots in the dust, my hands hanging there useless, the shed swaying about me. Stay, don't move, don't go. A fantasy, only a fantasy, only pretend. But the rifle barrel, it is hot, the powder smell, the ringing in my ears.

I must go out there, I must, before Papaíto comes up from the river, sees his only son frozen in the dust. And family, friends, school. Am I to be the blooded hunter-warrior, proud of his first kill.

I swagger into the sun, arms swinging stiffly, whistle a scrap of a tune—in case Papá sees me, in case I see me. My kill, beyond the kapok tree, lying on his side. A leg twitches, his chest heaves, blood bubbles from his mouth, his tongue hangs in the dust. Only a dark spot, a hole, below his ear. His eye turns to me. An inner light, soft, scared, asking why. It blinks once, opens wide, and, as if a cloud had drifted over us, its light is gone. His body sinks into the earth.

Papá comes to me, puts his arm across my shoulders, silent. I smell his breath, the blood, urine, the smoke from my cook fire. I rub my knuckles in my eyes.

A vulture spirals over us.

I, Ramiro, hungry. Orders for shoes are dwindling, my cobbling family's last few coins gone for the wages of their workers, for the hides in the shed gathering dust. Cobblers in the big towns, they're dyeing their leather now, German chemicals, new processes, the women crazed by the colorful choices. I'm back with the wagon half full. Los Etchos shoes left for the dust.

I'd sold a few saddles, boots, chaparreras for the vaqueros, that is all. Maybe a bridle or two, though mostly they use hemp, make their own jáquimas and mecates. The parade tack for the high-stepping stallions on Revolution Day, all shiny with silver medallions and tassels, the carved silver curb bits, the silver spurs with the tooled leather reins and straps, the shiny boots with the inlays of bright colors, all that comes from the city now—their machines and dyes and foreign skills.

The silver mines are closed down. No ore, no jobs. A worldwide war threatening. The grand houses, lush patios, arcades. Empty. Four-poster beds, pianos, golden chandeliers abandoned, useless. Los Etchos left dying in the dust.

~

Books, hijo mio, books. Enough of shoes. School, study, learn, get on with it. Learn English, that's the key. Put your head to work. And show up what's left of those Ricardos, those pálidos. You'll have to get out and earn the money. Tuition, room and board when you get to university, travel. Books, Ramiro, books. We have no savings, we cannot help.

My Mamá, she runs our lives. Tough as javalina meat, sweet too, though, sweet as the juice of the prickly nopal. She and the javalinas, they love the nopal fruit.

Tripping on the cobblestones, her dying feet, ulcerous, gray, numb. She leads me up the street. A ruined portal, a rotting door, its carvings cracked, meaningless. She pushes it open. A patio, a dead etcho, weeds, the well a tumble of stones. Two sides are high walls, the stucco crumbling, two sides are rooms. We push through a blanket covering a doorway into . . . a surprise for Ramiro!

My own, my study room, my bedroom. Freshly painted white, even the ceiling, the one part of the ruin with a roof still intact. A barred window, a fireplace, desk, cot, spirits lamp, three books.

Bless you, my Mamaíta. Herewith my path that you have led me to. From saddles and shoes to books, to learning, to telling, to teaching. To being a maxi me.

I hug you, I kiss your tears.

I have news. I start tomorrow as the weekend driver of the Tourist Train. A regular wage, good tips. Help for you and Papá.

~

Ramiro! Ramiro! A girl's voice, gentle, just there in the shadows across my room. Faint moonlight in my window, the shadow of palm leaves swaying ever so slightly on the wall. And there, a presence, a motion in the darkness? Ramiro, listen, listen carefully, I . . . Her voice fades, a whisper, silence. She has gone.

The next night, Wake up, Ramiro, listen. Your fireplace, under the embers, the ashes, dig, dig deep. I am half sitting, propped on my elbows. A stormy night, no light from my window, no shadows. I can see nothing, no faintest form, yet there, that presence, that shift of the darkness, that touch of warmth in the night air, that voice of a girl.

No fear, no questions, no doubts, no dreams.

Out into a sunny morning, the wet cobbles steaming, the palm leaves shining, the dust washed away. To breakfast with my parents. Talk of ghosts, their doubts. Stories, stories.

I go back to my new home, step up to my decaying door, ready to lift and push. A voice. I turn to the greetings from my neighbor. An elderly man, bent, no longer able to ride his mule to tend to his brother's cattle. He too has found an almost rainproof room in the house adjoining mine. I sometimes hear when he sets his kettle on the hearth.

So, Miro, ha! You've found yourself a girl. I hear her in there, two nights now.

His leer is pathetic.

I push though into my patio, sit on a stone bench in

the weeds. I shiver, I shut my eyes. Did he hear her instructions? Dig, I must, quickly, just in case.

I scrape the embers and ashes out onto the hearth. The fireplace floor is loose crumbling adobe brick, not fire bricks. I pull them out. The earth is loose, I can scoop it out with my hands. Maybe two handspans down I come to something hard. Metal, a handle, a pot top. I leave the lid on, dig down and around. It's all I can do to lift the vessel out, a heavy old stew pot. I dust it off, carefully lift off the lid.

Silver. Spanish coins, hundreds and hundreds of reales. All of them new as if just minted, though tarnished by time. And some bits of silverware too. Tiny cups with their dainty spoons, forks, knives, two snuff boxes.

That voice, that presence in my room last night. That motion in the dark, was it a figure, was it my lady of the deep green cloak?

I empty the pot onto the canvas sheet stamped with an iguana design that I use as a bedspread. The pot goes back under the fireplace floor, earth, bricks, ashes embers back in place. The canvas I draw together into a bag, sling it over my shoulder, carry it to my Papá. For Mamá, her medicines, her doctor, the surgeon when it is time, new feet for her, can they do that? And maybe a house for her in the city near the hospital? Please.

Welding, riveting, soon we're launching a troop transport, a Liberty ship, every five days. Thousands of us, men and women, swarming over the shipways. Enormous cranes swing in sheets of steel, thunderous gonging, clanked into position by dangling men. The welders, they're mostly women. More careful than men, they say, more aware of the dangers of sloppy work to the survival of the ship. They hang in their webs of electric cables. The crackle and dazzle of their arcs, the ozone stink, the smoke.

A fragile target for a torpedo, a tomb? The Nazi U-boats are sinking several of these a week.

Many of us come from across the border. We live in old warehouses made into barracks. A huge mess hall, a make-do basketball court, an emergency hospital under tents. Soon they have me interpreting to Spanish, training welders in the beginners' shed.

A woman's voice. Ramiro, is it truly you?

Her eyes catch mine, bright, smiling eyes. She looks down, she brings three fingers to her cinnamon lips, hiding that hint of a giggle. A hug, dare I? The ghost of a kiss to each cheek? Or just this mumble and sputter, quickly becoming a flood of our chattering voices tumbled together. Neighboring workers hear us in the din, stop to listen and laugh. The local quiet alerts us, alerts the supervisor. Embarrassed, we're back to work.

Can she like me, this tall and beautiful Lorena, this Mayo Yoreme woman? Me, this lumpy awkward Iguanito me?

That schoolmate girl, her warm smile for me across our schoolroom. A few words. Later, we are shooting hoops together once or twice. Ungainly kids, no more.

Let's hop a bus to the city.

Tacos, even here in the north, and dark faces, Spanish, ranchero music. We dance, a careful distance between us. We laugh, we look into each other's eyes, we come together. We feel, we explore. Our eyes, our bodies, our dreams.

Los Etchos still dusty. We're returning, men, women. One by one, from the shipyards, the flying fortress assembly lines, the Sherman tank testing grounds. Some had gone north to sign up in their army. They had fought the Japs and Jerry face to face, and some stayed on as career soldiers or new citizens.

Some like Ricardo were killed.

In 1942 our president declared war. Ricardo signed up in our Air Force, was trained as a pilot, and was sent to Texas with a squadron to be trained in Thunderbolt fighters. A few hundred of them, thirty pilots and their support, were shipped to the Philippines. In those last months of the war they fought the Japanese Zeros alongside the Americans. They marched as heroes through the streets of our capital. Ricardo and four other pilots went missing.

Lorena and I, we came back to Los Etchos together. We were put through some remnants of the traditional courtship rites. The, Señor Esquer, may I have the honor?

Married. Ramiro, Lorena Esquer de Valenzuela.

My pay check as a Master Specialty Welder had been very substantial and had usually gone straight into my bank account. Now I am ready and able to go back to the books. Two years of university, far from home and Lorena. We can't afford to have her join me. But there are the many tween-term weeks spent back in Los Etchos. Time for pickup jobs. Tour guide for the growing stream of visitors, interpreter, tutoring English. And my Lori.

She's there, on the edge of the field, watching some of us reunited schoolmates. They're friendlier now, or at least better mannered, in a shorthanded baseball game. I pitch, we lose. And Mamá is gone, no lotion. And so it is Lorena massaging my shoulder.

She takes my hand, we walk back into town together. Los Etchos shows signs of new life. A few Americans, mostly old folks seeking relief from wartime austerity, had settled here during the war. Buying several of the dozens of abandoned homes, they managed to get them renovated. A stone mason, a carpenter or two, were still in the town. A few families come back from the campo. Abandoned brick and tile ovens reopen, adobe blocks formed and set out to bake in the sun. Rotting amapa beams replaced. Roofs, bathrooms, fireplaces, up-to-date kitchens, replanted weedy patios. Everything repainted white. My Abuela works part time in one of those homes cleaning, cooking, tidying. Lori and I live with her now.

Peacetime, and more cheap-cost-and-sun seekers come. A hotel is reopened, another is created by combining several of the old abandoned mansions into one. For the ranchers the price of beef has been good, and many of them have been busy growing marijuana in the back country, now that it's illegal.

There, Señor Corbata. Whenever we see him he's wearing a necktie. He walks past us. Well-pressed suit, double breasted, old fashioned, maybe a bit threadbare. Shiny white shirt, the necktie held in place with a silver stickpin. He appears to live in a room, maybe a caretaker's room, in one of these houses brought back to life. It's only two or three doors down the cobbled street from Abuela's. He emerges every day in the early afternoon, siesta time, out through the arcades. We greet him, he gestures an acknowledgment, but we've never heard him speak. He walks off, always in the same direction. And he always returns at sunset. Where, why, who? No one seems to know. Small town curiosity. This is a neighbor, not a tourist.

An idea, Ramiro. I'll get Moscoso, my brat brother, to sneak after him, see where he goes every day.

Moscoso reports back. Corbata goes to a particular house, number thirty-seven, on the edge of town, an area where families moving in from the ranches have built a whole new barrio of small adobes.

We go mid-morning to avoid Corbata. His house still has plastic sheets instead of glass in the two windows, but the plastic is torn and yellowed, some years old. Pequeñitos playing in the dust, toddlers and crawlers, almost naked. Two of them are blond and blue-eyed. We walk by casually, and on back home.

Here in this poorest of barrios? Impeccably dressed, middle-aged, even an hidalgo or military bearing? Silent to our greetings in Spanish? We must find out. Let's try Moscoso again. Yes, your brother may be a brat, but he's smart, and good with people of all ages. A couple of his schoolmates live out there. What reward might we dangle before them?

We promise a baseball mitt, and he's out there the next day. With a few bits of candy he connects with two of the older kids, asks them who is the old man, the corbata man, I saw him coming here yesterday? All he got was a name, Tio Kurt.

More days, more visits. No luck connecting with any adult. Tio Kurt, that's all we get for an almost new mitt? Two days later, I'm out on our quiet street buying bread buns from one of the boys who carry their wares around on rickety wooden trays balanced on their heads. Señor Corbata appears, makes signs that he would like to buy one bun. He is having difficulty understanding the price. In English I say, Can I help you, sir?

He turns to me, silent for a moment, seems to stiffen, makes an ever so slight bow, and then: Yes, thank you, mister. Thick, mushy accent, but he does seem to know a bit of English.

With no forethought, I ask him in English if he would like me to help him learn Spanish. Again silence, a long close look at me, top to bottom, eye-to-eye, laboriously groping for words, he says yes, he would be interested, but would first like to learn about me and what I propose.

There's a stone bench under the arcade. I gesture toward it. We sit there, one at each end, and I slowly tell him, pausing between sentences to see if he understands me, that I now have a degree in English, that I tutor students in English and one or two recent arrivals from California in Spanish, that I have six weeks vacation from university, that I could work with him regularly, even daily, that I have only one last term at the university and would then be free to work with him more if he chooses.

Again a long pause, time enough for him to reach into a breast pocket, pull out a silver cigarette case, hold it open toward me, Thank you, I do not smoke. He lights up with a waxen match, then, word by painful word, pulled, I'd guess, from some distant schoolboy memory, always looking me straight in the eye, he gives me his reply in English.

First, he introduces himself formally. Kurt von Praunheim. He would like to have my help, but he has no money. I make out that he may have something of considerable value to offer me but the details are vague, I'm confused. But my interest is piqued. First he would like two trial sessions with me and I agree.

Sitting on that same bench, our third session. He has brought a black cloth bag, something small and heavy in it, sets it down carefully on the bench between us. Everything he does and says is with great care. Apologetic for being a slow learner but quite satisfied with our trials, he wishes to continue with daily sessions for the next six weeks if I am willing to accept this as payment. He hands the bag to me, I open it. In old but polished brown leather holsters are two formidable looking pistols. Familiar? Maybe from pictures, but I know nothing about firearms, have not touched one since the light faded from that stag's eye, a gangly kid in the mountains with his Papá.

He says, most haltingly: They are Lugers, the famous German military sidearm since before World War I. Lugers have become collectors items. Five cows were offered for one. Ammunition, I have only one magazine, but it is quite available, it's sold in at least two powers. Get the most powerful, the weaker power is not always enough to fully drive the fold-up bolt, not like the sliding bolts or revolving chambers of most pistols. So, will this do for payment?

Five cows, ten! Enough to buy you fluent Spanish, Señor, and much much more. Where did you get them?

That, Señor Ramiro, is a story for another time. When you are back from your studies you might be so kind as to accompany me on a short trip. I will tell you the story then.

Lorena, I hear her steps behind me, she comes around the kitchen table. She stands for a moment, that lovely smile, looking down at me. My beautiful Mayo, dark, slender, the shining black hair, a lock escaping from her folded bandana. From my smile, her eyes look down on the bag lying before me on the table. Her raised eyebrow, the tilt of her head, curious, questioning. She undoes the top button of her jeans. A bit of dark skin over her growing belly. pulls out her chair, sits.

He's paid me, our Señor Corbata, our Kurt von Praunheim, more than I'd ever dreamt, far more than enough to go on teaching him Spanish for years, I tell her. No no, don't be alarmed, he is learning fast, careful, diligent, keen. Here, open it, there are ten steers in that bag and the price of beef is the highest ever.

Yes, two pistols, Lugers, he calls them Parabellum Pistolen too, not loaded, and no, I'm still your sane and steadfast pacifist. In fact one pistol really is no longer mine. I am trading it for... But come, I'll show you. Here, take my hand. Wait, I'll tie your bandana over your eyes. Trust me, two steps down. Slow now on the cobblestones. No, wait. I'll turn you around, once, twice, again. Quite befuddled, yes? Now come.

Stop, half a step, there, now three up. Hold on to me. Cooler here, dark, where can we be? Lighter again, the purring of doves, a breeze stirring above. Soft earth, dust in your sandals, warm in your toes, no? Where can we be? Now, we stop here. Reach out, both hands, I'll place them, just here. And off with the bandana.

Heart-shaped vine leaves, as big as corn tortillas. Climbing my Mango Tree, our Mango Tree. Here in the patio, our new home.

I bought it yesterday from Elena Valdez, Donna Raquel's great granddaughter. Remember her from school? Tucked in here between the crumbling arcades of two once elegant mansions. A stable once, maybe? Three rooms. Half the roof to redo, maybe pave the patio with bricks some day. The well collapsed years ago, Elena told me. We'll dig it out, a bucket on a pulley or maybe a pump if it's not too deep.

What is Lorena's reaction to all this?

A coffee, Lorena mia? That's Donna Raquel's old kitchen, there under the tin-roof shed beyond Mango. Just those bricks, the grill, mango twigs and branches, mesquite logs. The pot should be hot, waiting for us.

Your mug. Come sit by me, here where I, little Ramiro, would settle between Mango's root shoulders, lean against her trunk. Where I'd be with my dreams. The Virgen of Guadalupe in her aura, in her starry cloak of green, she was up there in those branches. Her dove came to show me where to dig, here in the dust, for this, my tiny iguanita spoon dangling on its thong.

I, Mango Tree, once but a bit of green on moist earth, a tiny leaf, roots reaching down. In the warm arms of the sun, soon dancing to the wind. Now, old friends leaning against me, a new one in their arms. Welcome to me, to this home that fills the sky, to the multitudes living with us here.

We leave Los Etchos before dawn, Señor Corbata and I. This is to be the short trip he had promised. He has been working hard on his already quite adequate Spanish, but was close-mouthed about this trip.

Good boots, Ramiro, a hat, something warm for a night out in a shelter. Bring water, bread, cheese, dried meat, a mostly empty sack. No word as to just where we are headed or why the sacks.

Kurt flashlights the path. Cold night air flows down the mountainside rising a thousand meters above us. A dog barks on the far side of town, a rooster manages a half-hearted call, a burro just over the fence scolds his empty bucket.

Monte Plateado, our silver mountain, silvery cliffs in the full moon. Evenings it would be angry in a baleful setting sun. Foreboding, ever lowering over Los Etchos, its name foretells the greed of the colonizers for its ore. Rapine, wealth, and misery.

By the time the sun appears over the range far to the southeast we are climbing the steep stream bed well above the last ranch. A band of coatis, they race through the tree tops, silencing the purr of a mourning dove. Señor Kurt, he's ahead. Long strides when the track levels, heavy boots he said he'd bought in the market, worn but with a good tread. Jeans, a flannel shirt, an anorak, a visored cap, no necktie. He stops, swings his sack off his shoulder, steps over to sit in the shade of the last of the pines, only the winter-dry leafless forest and the etchos and cactuses below. I join him, sit on my half full sack, steaming, rocks paling in the sun.

Still saying little, Kurt points out our route. On up, ever steeper, climbing on the narrowing scar of bare rocks which the Mayo Yoreme would call a water serpent sliding down the mountainside.

Beyond the tip of our serpent's tail, and on over that gap between those two sentinel peaks, mi Profesor, down the other side a short way, rocks and talus, to the edge of a pine forest.

A rigorous route of many hours, and I have no idea still what the trip may offer. Somehow, though, I accept this enigmatic man, his contained and disciplined manner, his eyes that search into me and offer an exchange of trust. A sad man, but with self-assurance and clearly familiar with the route ahead. I had often been in mountains around Los Etchos with my father, with schoolmates, or alone. But I knew of no one who had been up and over Plateado. There is an unspoken taboo, a legend, a fear of those water serpents that have poured their torrential wrath on mountain people over the ages.

We set off up that slithery back, silver-white in the morning sun, slippery, wet from last night's dew. By the original people of the mountain, there are five serpents, rocky watercourses, gods of our mountain. Their tails near the jagged summit, winding down, cascading past cliffs, through forests, ranches, homes. Gorged bellies.

We are over the top by early afternoon, exhausted, sweaty. We slide down a few hundred feet of loose shale talus. At the base of a sentinel peak is an opening in the cliff face. A cave. And a few feet below it there is a patch of green. A slope of grass, a scrub of willow, a spring there where the stunted pines begin.

As we approach the opening, Kurt signals for silence, caution. We keep to the side. Out of sight of any occupant of the cave, is that what he's doing? He holds a hand to his mouth, makes a sharp whistle. I know it, the rock squirrel's danger signal. A tasty tidbit for a predator. Jaguar, mountain lion, bobcat, javelina, a vicious badger? We wait, he whistles again. Nothing. He moves closer, tosses a rock near the entrance. Nothing. With his flashlight held to one side, away from his body, he steps into the opening and disappears. Long minutes later there's a low scraping sound echoing from deep within the cave. Soon he is back, calling me to come in.

I follow the circle of his light on the cave floor, his boots puffing the dust. A few feet in, the light slides up the rock wall, stops on the petroglyph of an antlered buck. Further, the cave widens into a small room. Slabs of rock fallen from the walls and ceiling piled to one side.

A fire pit, a blackened crack in the ceiling, a glimmer of light. Stacked firewood, two small crude wooden chests, benches of logs, mats of palm fronds. The light swings to the back wall, to a flat rock that has been dragged, rolled aside, scuffing the dust, uncovering an opening, an enlarged crack in the wall. Is there a glimmer there too, does the crack go through to another entrance? Kurt's light picks out a form lying there, bulky with…? A twitching tail, a sabertooth? Kurt kneels, reaches for the tail, hands it to me.

Here, pull out that sack. We'll take it out into daylight. And with it, my story too.

A bit of ledge, mossy, moist, a trickle dripping into a brimful rusty bucket half buried in the earth. A spider dancing on the surface, hoverflies. A blueing butterfly lights on a leaf floating in the bucket and sips. Two overgrown vegetable beds, a few bolted brassicas, a patch of marijuana lost in the weeds.

Kurt opens the sack. Two more in the cave to sort out later, he tells me.

In the dry bufflegrass he arranges six Luger pistols, eight pairs of black jackboots, five caps, three high-peaked hats, one of them with a white cover. And a small metal box. Insignia, medals, swastika armbands. He stands up, steps back, heels together in the dust, back held straight, his face rigid and sad.

Unterseeboot Kapitanleutnant Kurt von Praunheim.

His shoulders sag. His story begins in clipped Spanish, precise, disciplined.

Born into the German military, my father was an officer in the World War One Kaiserliche Marine. After the surrender, for more than a decade Germany was being bled to death by the Treaty of Versailles. Hitler and his National Socialist Party brought hope, self-esteem, pride, purity, redemption. Respect, duty, power, hatred. The Vaterland.

1939. War.

Kurt von Praunhiem, a young officer in the Kriegsmarine, already finished a five years training program for Unterseeboot duty. The fleet of U-boats is growing fast. On my first patrol, I, Second Watch Officer von Praunheim, am in charge of the watchcrew on deck, the Flak gun and the deck gun, and the radio room crew. A month in the north Atlantic, mostly lying in wait for the easy targets, the neutrals, ducking their warships, their planes. Eleven sinkings.

Later long patrols in bigger submarines, soon as Kapitanleutant, ranging America's east coast, the Caribbean, refueled, resupplied by the enormous unarmed Milchkühe subs. Diesel, water, food, fresh bread, mail.

In late 1944, still miraculously alive and on home furlough, I am called to Unterseebooten headquarters in Berlin. An officer on Admiral Dönitz's staff hands me an envelope, tells me to read its instructions carefully, now, memorize it. I'll wait. When you're ready, we'll burn it.

You will follow it precisely tomorrow morning at eleven. Now burn it here, a match, here in this ash tray.

A hotel lounge, two chairs in a corner, a rather ordinary man in civilian dress, reading a two-days-old Berlin newspaper to identify him. I hand him a current newspaper as my identity. We walk to a nearby park, sit on a bench in an open deserted area. In clipped brief sentences I am entrusted with perhaps the most sensitive and dangerous mission of the war.

I am to take command of a new, specially designed VIIC submarine at the Bergen U-boat base. St. Nazaire has held out against the enemy's invasion of France, but cannot be supplied and can no longer serve us as our principal submarine base.

In order to increase its range, in place of all but two torpedoes, this elongated version of the VIIC has extra fuel tanks, water tanks, and provision storage. It had been planned to use the larger long range VIIF torpedo supply submarine, but the last survivor of the four commissioned VIIFs, the U-1062, was lost somewhere off the Cape Verde Islands. The U-boat will be designated as U-133, though U-133 was actually sunk off Salamis, Greece, in 1942. The reason for this subterfuge will become clear, but at the core it was anonymity, an untraceable escape from the meticulous archives of the German military.

I'm told that this new U-133 will be loaded with four small but very heavy, sealed metal containers marked as Experimental Solid Nuclear Fuel. I am ordered to sail as soon as possible to join the German Monsun Gruppe of U-boats based at the Japanese submarine base in Penang, on the Straits of Malacca. En route refueling rendezvous from tankers, probably in the regions of the Cape Verde Islands and Mauritius, will be arranged by enciphered radio. U-133 will be the forty-second U-boat sent to the Indian Ocean and the Pacific, though few have made it all the way. The Indian Ocean has been for a time a good hunting ground for German and Japanese submarines. Shipping lanes were largely unprotected. But the U-133 must avoid all possible contact with enemy or neutral ships of any kind. The torpedoes are to be used only in an extreme emergency.

U-133 will refuel and resupply in Penang. My crew will be reduced there to a minimum. I am in agreement with this secret headquarters that since the mission is not military, the usual complement of forty-four could be cut to about sixteen, thus reducing sleeping space, torpedo space, and the consumption of oxygen. It will add supply space, making room for more fuel in supplementary tanks and barrels. The other crew members will be reassigned to U-boats in the area. With these measures and with reduced speeds to achieve maximum fuel efficiency, the range of U-133 will be about doubled, more than enough to fulfill the mission. We have no milk-cow submarines or tankers in the Pacific.

On arrival at the mission's destination, the U-133 was to be scuttled within rowing distance of the coast but in reasonably deep waters. No one from the U-133 will be returning to the Fatherland until the end of the war.

When we arrive in Penang, we get radio instructions as to exact destination and rendezvous time. We have agents throughout Latin America. Pursuant to our orders, the designated agent will be ready to receive us and direct us.

The officers and crew would leave U-133 on three life rafts. I and seven crew members will go first. Those seven men are designated on the crew list as Spanier. They have been assigned and were already on board the U-133 when I took command. When war began and it was decided that Spain would be declared officially neutral, many men of the Spanish Navy volunteered for German U-boat duty. These seven were chosen as the best and most experienced of Spanish-speaking U-boat submariners.

The other two life rafts, each under the command of one of the two remaining officers with half of the remaining crew, each loaded with two of the metal containers, would await a light signal from me on the shore that they should proceed with the scuttling and come in to the shore. The four metal containers will be delivered to the agent and the local authorities who will accompany him. Transportation of the boxes will probably be by mule.

There may be several days of walking in difficult terrain. I, as Kapitan, will be advised by the agent and the local officials, but will continue to be in command of the crew.

Before disembarking from U-133, each member of the crew would wash and shave. Razors and saltwater soap will be provided each will change into summer-weight shore-duty uniform with rank and service insignia, and the appropriate headgear and boots. Each man would wear his identification disc, and carry a personal knapsack containing a Luger with two ammunition magazines, casual rough civilian-style work clothes, and rations of sufficient water and food for several days.

I had been briefed of the origins and the objectives of this mission. There are authorities in Berlin charged with assessing the strategies and progress of the war. They operate in complete secrecy. For some time they have concluded that Germany may soon have to admit defeat. If this were to happen, it is the mission of the U-133 to help in finding and nurturing new soil where the ideals of National Socialism can take root and flourish, a land that can harbor many of our wise leaders taking refuge there who can help in the fostering of this revival. Those metal boxes contain gold ingots to enable this cause.

There was to be no written record of this mission at least until it is completed.

This Señor Kapitan Kurt, he is sitting cross-legged now by the drip-drip of the tiny spring. One hand is on his knee, the other plays idly with a small silver object on a silver neck chain. He stares at the rippled surface of that circle of water. A yellow leaf falls on the surface, a bluewing lands. The leaf darkens as the moisture soaks through, the bluewing flutters off. Slowly turning, the leaf sinks out of sight.

He looks up, eyes steady on mine, a hint of a tear. He unhooks the bit of silver from its chain, hands it to me. It is a small medallion, plain on one side, on the other inscribed with U-133.

He wipes a tear on his cheek, his body relaxes. He offers me a cigarette. We both blow rings with our first exhales. He lies on a patch of moss.

So long a voyage, so tedious, so many tense times waiting. We live with fear. Sinking to periscope depth, motors off, no voices, no movements, watching prime targets steam by. Creeping, on half-speed. Waiting at our rendezvous, plans disrupted. Battered by a typhoon, diving under it just beyond Mauritius.

Penang offers little respite. Greeted by atrocious renditions of our Horst-Wessel-Lied and the Japanese anthem. Our hosts are nervous, distant, rations are miserable, the population terrified, particularly the hated Chinese, mortal enemies to be persecuted at will by the occupying forces. There are almost daily air raids, British, American, Australian, their submarines attacking too. The Japanese are getting ready to abandon Penang, to relocate to Jakarta.

U-133 moves out quickly, having fueled up, resupplied, and winnowed the crew and officers down to sixteen.

To be the Kapitan of this mission, the sole bearer of its import, its implicit admission that the Deutsches Reich was defeated, its unlikely dream of a rebirth, its seemingly certain doom for U-133 and its crew. A heavy burden to bear alone. For a U-Boot to survive on simply a routine patrol was tenuous. The precise records were kept secret, but it was not difficult to keep some count. The casualty lists, the production quotas, word of mouth. By the time this reborn U-133 leaves Norway the guesses among us are that of the perhaps eleven hundred built since 1939, six hundred will not have survived, twenty thousand submariners dead.

Official news from Berlin. Glorious victories of a rapidly shrinking empire, London again devastated by V-1 and V-2 bombs, civilian heroics in smashed German cities even as they broadcast by day and by night that there are no enemy aircraft over the entire Vaterland. A war that has destroyed half the world. A hopeless war, by now an insane war. Yet with our radio we still hear the Sieg Heil victory cry of the Aryan race, the atrocious cheers for freedom from the yellow Star of David.

We received messages in Penang and again in Batavia giving destination details, slight changes and with information as to how and when to make radio contact with the destination agent. Four months after leaving Bergen, U-133 is approaching the Mexican coast. Intelligence radioed from Berlin reports that with the gradual retreat of the Japanese and their submarines, the Americans have shifted their naval defenses westwards, leaving the Pacific coast of the continent only lightly patrolled. Since leaving New Zealand waters, U-133 has seen few ships or aircraft. The problems now relate more to local navigation and to making final contact with the agent. We enter the Sea of Cortez, sail north, largely submerged. Waiting until dark, with the coordination of radar, depth sounding, and radio direction findings on the agents radio signals, U-133 slips through a row of mangrove islands a mile and a half off the Mexican coast, and anchors off an uninhabited Sonoran beach.

Shaved, dressed in our uniforms, Lugers prominent in their holsters, I and the seven Spaniers step out onto the beach, into the lights of several flashlights. The crew's flashlights in turn pick out a middle-aged man, balding, paunchy, dressed in rough work clothes. He holds out his hand, greeting us in English and Spanish. Obligingly lit now by this agent's flash light, is a muddy jeep and, standing by it, three men. The light goes from one to another. Dark skinned, in black uniforms, with various rank insignia on their epaulettes. The one with the most stars wears a more authoritative hat than the simple caps of the other two. For a moment they shield the light with a hand, then salute, Bienvenido, señor capitán. The agent begins to talk in Spanish, the U-133 radio operator taking on the role of translating into German.

These officers say they represent very important leaders of the country's government. They offer honored asylum to their visitors and to any member of the German Republic verified by intelligence staff. The ideals and goals of National Socialism must not die. They wish to show us a document which confirms, with signatures, their leaders' intent. They will ask you to sign it, with a copy for yourself, when they have received the cargo that U-133 has brought.

The agent is a nervous man, unsure of himself, his eyes forever escaping. He glances twice out to sea, but there is nothing to be seen, no lights, no ships. In the faint starlight, only the white tips of waves coming in on the strand in a growing wind, splashing over the stern of the beached life raft.

Assured that this is an uninhabited stretch of coast and that there are no fishermen out there in this weather, the radioman is ordered to light a flare, aiming it out to sea.

Hours pass, nothing. Through a long night, nothing. With dawn, distance comes to life, but nothing, no black form out there, low and sleek, no blueish rafts bringing in the protection payments. I and three of the crew shove our raft back into the sea, row out to the area where they had anchored. Nothing. They circle around, systematic, ever widening circles. Throughout the morning, nothing. Midday, distant shouts from the shore, they row back. A body has washed up, the Leutnant zur See second watch officer, drowned. No raft, no gold. No document to sign, no deal.

The three black uniforms move to the far side of the jeep, quiet talk, glances at the agent and the eight summer uniforms of khaki. No further word, the three in uniform drive off in the jeep, leaving the agent cursing, gesticulating, crushed. He turns to me, his pate an angry pink, his eyes still searching for escape, his voice a splutter, interpreted.

A disaster, we are all in danger, no telling how those men will react, who they'll report to. You and your men, Kapitan, could be treated as spies since this country reluctantly and late in the war joined the Allies. That is why your instructions were to land in your uniforms. Now, without the quasi-official protection of those federal police officers and their document, you'd be safer, less conspicuous, in your civilian work clothes, though carrying your uniforms and IDs in case you are caught and held as probable spies. The contingency plan for you in the event of mishap is to proceed on foot to that mountain range, there to the east, you can see it. To Monte Plateado, high on its uninhabited south side, a cave, a small spring, some provisions. No one goes there, the locals seem to be afraid of it, and it's impossible terrain for cattle. And you have your side arms. Here, this contour map, I've marked the route, Plateado, the cave. Three days hike should do it. I am required, now, to leave you.

He simply scurries away.

A German, seven Spaniards, dry desert, faint blue mountains to the northeast, it must be a good fifty kilometers. The map shows the highest peak, this Monte Plateado, as something more than two thousand meters. Compass reading, corrected for variation, will be about twenty degrees.

Change clothing, men, pocket your pistols out of sight. Dusk, it's a good time to head off. Best leave the body where it is, on the beach, untouched, uniform and all. One more mystery for officialdom if it is found. If we meet anyone, you men are recent arrivals from Spain, refugees. You hear there are logging jobs in the mountains. I'd be a German refugee.

Five nights, it was, then a last struggle in the brutal sun climbing this monstrous mountain, searching for this cave, this bucket of water.

Dust, the stink of urine, of diesel fumes, rattling through the potholes and the speed-bump topes and vibradores, inside this rusted wreck of a bus, my weekly ordeal. Years of torment, the journey from Los Etchos to Universidad, weekdays rooming with a cousin in his dilapidated shack, and back weekends to my waiting, willing Lorena.

Lorena, insistent, she would laugh at my doubts, willing me to study, to learn a career, to take us someday from subsistence to comforts, to that other world that dazzles just over some horizon. You must, Ramiro.

My Lori, working as full-time secretary to the mayor, but she wants more. We both do. I close my eyes.

I wake into dates and names and the greed of history. Into two languages becoming one. Two obsessions, two studies, two lives. Am I mad? The histories of these lands, their souls, their tongues that tie us together and hold us apart. Could that obsession carry us out of Los Etchos? Might it take us farther, across borders, oceans, over that horizon? The will, the energy, a good memory, a good ear, my family. Those are my assets. And my Lugers. One that bought our house, the other is always with me, my totem. Here, I feel its bulk in my rucksack on the seat beside me.

A dream: I am in a forest. The Luger, the Parabellum Pistole, is in its holster on my hip. I unbuckle the leather flap, withdraw the pistol. It shines in the bits of sun that pierce the leafy canopy. A handful of cartridges loose in my pocket, I load eight into the grip, pull up and back on the toggle breechblock, release to ready, flip the safety. Eight cans on a rock, medium range. Eight shots, eight cartridges ejected, cluttering the dust, eight cans gone.

A jolt, I edge out of sleep. That second Luger, here beside me. Collateral, a reserve asset, a potential response to violence? No. Contrarily, its closeness assures me, it will never be used. Moral encouragement, a presence, an enabler of fulfillment? Yes. But it stays with, it stays in its holster, the flap with the swastika imprint always buckled tight. This I swear to my Lori, to this me, to the dying light in the questioning eye of my stag.

I'm drifting in the stacks of the immense University library. Free, wandering through opinions and facts and truths and lies. If it weren't for Lori waiting for me under our Mango Tree, I'd spend my days there in that endless network of minds. Me, Ramiro, the cobbler's son, the dark-skinned Iguaníto, the stag slayer, the keeper of the Parabellum Luger and its secrets.

I look to the horizons. With my English–Spanish certificate, my history degree, my doctoral dissertation, published too, I am Doctor Ramiro Valenzuela. With Lori okay in English, shipbuilding lingo a speciality. An accomplished welder. Not half bad either side of an office desk. And now with our baby, our little Ceci about to be born. Toot my horn. Jobs, applications, whatever, wherever. Maybe Gringoland, or on around the globe.

Another trip to the Universidad, trapped in this sagging bus. I'll dig in the library over the weekend. Periodicals, job announcements, addresses, catalogs, professors, lecturers, course offerings. Hopefully college level, and I'll take aim at the U.S. and Canada for now. And on Monday, school leave-time to be phoned in by Lori, I'll visit the consulates, see what the problems will be. Passports, visas, family, quotas, letters of support, evidence of this and that, work permits, timing.

By Lorena's command, we have pulled a cot out under Mango Tree, here by our hammocks. All is ready. An ancient crib newly painted, we've padded the inner sides with bits of a salvaged blanket, a mosquito net over the top, a folded quilt for a mattress. Diapers ready, this-and-that things the women have assembled. The nearby doctor alerted. Abuela moved into the back room, ready with her midwifery. Kettle simmering as the gasps of labor begin.

I have seen the pictures, heard the birthing screams in our neighborhood. But my Lori? The delight, the ecstasy of that lovely body. A body to be torn, the blood, the shrieks? From sweet embrace to agony, to terror, to glimpses of death.

To our child.

Our Cecilia, our Ceci. The remnants of brutal birth are swept clean by the miraculous presence of this daughter. Her dark eyes that look so intently into ours, first her Mother's, then Father's, then Abuela's weeping in her happiness. This tiny being from us, knowing us, she turns to that loveliest of all forms, her mother's breast.

# PART 2

Another high school assembly. We the teachers, melting in the sun, half dozing. This time the standard-carriers are preceded by a line of boys bashing drums, and a second line blasting on trumpets with the two or three notes they could manage. I squint, the scene fades through a haze of eyelashes. Floating there in the shimmer, a slow dance, my six applications in their neat envelopes, stamped, postmarked, ready. And off they go. Drifting over mountains, deserts, beaches, seas of white-topped waves, ignoring borders. On, more mountains, deserts, towns and cities, campuses. Dignified brick buildings, Greek columns, modern glassy buildings, everything air-conditioned. Eager faculties admiring me?

My daily stop at our post office, squeezed into a corner of our dilapidated municipal hall, dark, its one window shaded against the sun, cool with its thick adobe walls. Two long envelopes, metered U.S. stamps, logos, one a college, one a university. My hand trembles as I slide them into my jacket pocket. Home, a bench under

Mango Tree, Lori beside me, Ceci playing with yellow leaves in the dust. I carefully slit the envelopes open with my pocket knife.

A polite form letter No from the university.

A Yes from the college.

We shout, we dance around Mango Tree, we dry joyful tears with the backs of our hands. We celebrate with glasses of Lori's special mango juice and milk mix.

The yes has several conditions and details. An interview in two weeks, travel expenses paid by the College, for the position in the next academic year as assistant professor in the History Faculty. Salary and prerequisites to be discussed. If accepted, on-campus family housing is available. Help will be offered in getting the appropriate visas including a letter stating that your unique qualifications are not available in United States. Several documents will be needed. Certified copies of your university records, police records checks, health exams for you and family. And so forth.

We look at the notes I made about Vermejo College. Vermejo, Arizona, in hill country on the edge of the high deserts. A four-year college for men and women, no postgraduate program, it is comparatively new and small. Several of the original faculty members were colleagues on the faculty of a large Eastern university who sought independence to try out new methods and areas of study. One relative innovation is the abolition of tenure, believing it to be stultifying. In the college's envelope of material, there's a current catalog which includes a discussion of their plans for a program of Latin American studies, including studies of indigenous peoples, to begin the succeeding year. Latin American studies had not generally been given much time in American colleges and universities. It seemed particularly appropriate to undertake this in an area close to the United States border with the Latin American world. And it speaks of their search for the appropriate teacher to join the History Department. Me?

When I had accepted the interview invitation, they sent me a generous money order for travel expenses and per diem. Two days, train, a bus, an overnight on a bus station bench to save the per diem for better use, another bus. The last half hour we've been climbing slowly out of the reddish Vermejo Desert, from tumbleweed and ocotillo to sage and creosote, up into mesquite, juniper, stunted oak. Pigs munching acorns, javelinas, roadrunner on into the ponderosas and meadows. Cattle grazing in the wildflowers, their shadows stretched out to the east. The beginnings of a town. Filling station, bowling alley, Mexican restaurant, a run-down DropInn motel, Vacancy. Fire station, two shiny engines outside being hosed down. Bashas, Your Hometown Grocer. A Studebaker dealer. Now the post office. Two boys are taking the flag off the halyard, stretching it out between them. I count six stars down, eight across. They are folding it in triangles toward each other.

Frame houses, mostly white with colored gingerbread, mowed grass to the sidewalks, flower beds, shrubs. Main

Street, brick buildings, shops, a small town square, shade trees, cast-iron fence and benches and bandstand that had somehow escaped the gluttonous wartime arms industry. At the far side of the square is the brick town hall and court house with its colonnaded entrance. And a block farther the Vermejo Hotel 1883: Restaurant & Bar, neon Schlitz in the window.

The bus stops. I climb down, walk back to the DropInn, register. My room stinks of mildew and cigarettes. I leave my hand bag, cross the street to the Restaurante: Mexican & American. Quesadillas and Pabst Blue Ribbon, early to bed.

The College is a few minutes walk up the slope back of the town hall. The centerpiece is a mansion. Brick painted white, two stories with a third level of dormers in a steep slate roof, a kind of turret in the middle, marble steps with stone lions on the balustrades up to the double front door. A cattle baron, or mining, railroad money, lumber, banking? Shade trees, lawns with sprinklers everywhere. A haze in the morning sun. Brick-walled acres, yet close to the middle of the town. Several two-story frame buildings here and there under the oaks and maples, plain, quite new, functional I'd guess. Students hurrying about, green book bags, slacks, shirttails—men and women.

An older woman, maybe fifty, comes toward me, skirt halfway down her calf. Is this the New Look for these Americans? Our women are all full-skirted, girls too. She'd be glad to show me the way to my interview appointment. That will be in Gibson Hall, that monstrous mansion there, HQ we call it. Yes, yes, I've heard about you. Good luck.

A young woman sits at the reception desk, may be a student even, the stereotype blond American girl. Welcome, Doctor Valenzuela, yes, the faculty has just arrived, they're in there with the Prez, I'll buzz him. She reaches over to the buzzer, but without looking. She's staring at me, looks surprised, my face, then my hands, palms. And smiles, an exaggerated smile, and stands up, holds out her hand, a hearty handshake, perhaps a bit prolonged.

My skin, my color. I'd lived with it, my own little world in Los Etchos, those years in California. I'd learned to expect new encounters with whites to be unnatural, to expect the first-off caution, the pulling back, the judgment. It's nice to get the opposite. Or is it, is it just the other side of the same coin? Ah well, and a green light flashes on her buzz pad. She goes over to the door, holds it open for me. Five or six men and women come forward. How will they see me?

The score, will I go through life keeping score. But does everyone, in any interaction? Four are surprised, then extra warm. Two, and they're older than the others. A glimpse, the eyes turn away, the body language is a drawing in, defensive–aggressive.

Coffee for all, we settle into a circle. Then the questions, personal at first, friendly, evolving into names and dates and trends, but clearly most interested in opinions. This Senator Allende in Chile, the White House, much of the media too, tag him as commie, concerned about his run for the presidency. What are your views? Argentina's Perón. To what extent would you say his admiration for

Mussolini influences his populist policies? What can you tell us of the Orozquista Rebellion in Sonora, its origins and justifications?

On and on. But the mood changes. It started as a kind of probing by at least several of the panel, to trip me up on facts, to evaluate my English, testing to see my leanings in historical analysis, catch me in extremism. Soon, though, it becomes cordial, an exchange of views and analyses among equals. The interview ends in affability.

Siesta time, I'm exhausted. Nerves, interview angst, culture shock, that student-guided tour of the campus did go on and on. And this waiting for the promised phone call.

I pick the phone up, put it on the bed beside me. Cracked plastic, sticky to feel, ashes and food bits stuck to the mouthpiece, DropInn style. I turn away from the window, close my eyes.

It rings. This is the college receptionist, a voice says. In a word, señor Ramiro, it looks to me like it's a Yes. And the president and his wife invite you for dinner at their apartment, sixish.

Thank you for the preview, and I accept the invitation with pleasure.

I close my eyes again, my right fist up, thrust forward ¡Estupendo! A Western Union telegraphed Yes! to Lori. I spend the afternoon in the College library digging through college catalogs, text books, and whatever I can find about how Latin American history is taught in the U.S.

Back to my beautiful Ceci, her waving black hair already long, her darkest eyes with flecks of laughing gold. Toddling, bubbling with her own language, only a year old. Making a game of finding her mother's breast. She examines a huge morpho butterfly resting in the bougainvillea. Stretching its wings, brilliant blue on the peach of the flowers. She raises her finger to touch it. No, my Ceci, she is so delicate, even a touch would hurt her, understand? Shall we show her to Mamá?

Lori, there by the cook fire, stirring a soup pot. She shakes bits of earth from her shiny black hair, covers the pot, looks up to curse and wink at a gecko scrambling among the sticks and crooked beams of our portales ceiling. He's snapping up his lunch of bugs. Our kitchen, a fire pit in a corner of the patio, smoky under the slanting roof. It's the driest corner, southwest, where the rains don't blow in. I must linseed oil the amapa columns before we go. Three of them, a liter should do.

Ceci's back at her construction project. Crisp yellow mango leaves crisscrossed into a precarious tower. I head for my bright green washroom, the opposite corner, there where old Ragbag tethered her donkey. I'd cobbled it together when we first moved in. Water barrel filled weekly with buckets from the town fountain, a basin, a shelf with our this-and-that, a covered seat over a deep hole, a vent pipe up through the roof, a can of lime.

A living room, some furniture from my parents when they sold their adobe two-room house, moved to the city.

And died so very soon.. Our bedroom, mattress on the floor, an ancient crib for Ceci. One room empty, a leaky roof. One Luger. And Mango Tree.

Once, maybe a hundred years ago, the mines still swarming with activity, a house like this might have been a wing of a mansion given to a son of a silver mine owner as a wedding present. In their living rooms, these families would store dozens of bars of silver for safety and no doubt for show too. They would make stacks of them as benches, covered with rugs and cushions, waiting there till a hundred-mule wagon caravan and its protecting private army could be assembled to take the silver to a Caribbean port. Many weeks over often wild and rugged terrain. Silver for the curches, the mansions, the palaces of Europe.

There is a story in Los Etchos that on a rainy wedding day the father of the bride had stepping stones made of these ninety pound bars of the silver stretched up and across a muddy street leading to the church.

Portraits, Steinway pianos, crystal chandeliers from Europe, chinoiseries, extravagant parties, imported delicacies. Patterned silks woven for these families by a group of Japanese in a complex of homes and patios. Mulberry trees, trays of silkworms, the straw frames, vats, reeling machines, spindles for the hand reeling of threads for the heavier materials, the looms. And the elaborate trappings, the icons, of their cattle ranches, rifles in their leather holsters inlaid with silver, the displays of shining spurs, branding irons, sombreros. Reminders too of the endless revolutions. Swords, uniforms, military decorations, pomp, legend... failure.

We still see remnants of that life in the abandoned mansions that have not been rebuilt. When I was in middle school, I picked up some piano skill on a decrepit Blüthner which I fixed up and figured out how to more or less tune. Pliers and a tuning fork I borrowed from our class teacher.

Sounds, smells, fading, quiet. Gone, those voices, their smoke, their clatter?

My myriad blossoms, tickled by the yellow hoverflies, blossoms that embrace me. Puffs of pollen in this lazy breeze. Doves returning, white wings, soft cooings. None of those two-leggeds waiting many suns for my fruit to ripen, readying to poke them loose with bamboo poles.

Yes, they have gone.

Ceci's creation grows, a zigzag across the carpeting until the Tinkertoy carton is empty. She pulls it apart, carefully scatters the sticks and spools. Not looking up, she seeks approval or disapproval, Mamá?

But it's Pá, me, here, not Má, monkey. Didn't you hear her splashing about in the bath? Let's put it all back in its box.

I'm *not* a monkey!

A church, there's no College church. Another of our founders' innovations. Our Los Etchos church would do that too, that fast bong-bong-bong for a couple of minutes, and later when everyone headed for the service has presumably arrived, a more dignified slow bonging. Polite greeting, or resignation at the low turnout of Los Etchenses.

With last splash from the bathroom and Lori is out, summoned to her worship. A walk and a picnic high in the beckoning hills.

Soon we had a car. Old, dented, rattly, they're servicing it and changing the tires for us now. Then we'll be off into the deserts. Navajo, Havasupai, Hopi country. The mountains, the canyons, pictured in every Vermejo shop and eatery.

But for now a walk, Ceci on my back. Ramiro, will you take her after our picnic? Up the hill behind the College, into sun and sky and beauty. Through a parkland of ponderosas. Higher into piñons, meadows of grasses, wildflowers. Blue lupine, scarlet paintbrush, yellow linaria, white poppies. A weaving of Gaia's altarpiece.

And beyond, where the aspen begin, their leaves quaking light and dark green, their trunks are signposts. On their white bark, scars in fours and fives, high up, a bear marks his territory. Slashes, an elk's nibbling teeth, a stag scraping the velvet from his new antlers. In a sunny opening in the aspen, we spread out our raggedy lap rug, big enough for the three of us in one hammock, like those chilly evenings under Mango Tree. Bread, cheese, two cans of Dos Equis, apple juice for Ceci, a bunch of grapes. The three of us stretch out, doze to the distant drone of cicadas in the ponderosas.

Or maybe it's stormy and cold, snow needles that sting, everything a dim white blur. We'd stir the embers in our tiny fireplace, add split mesquite logs, pull up our armchairs, park Ceci between us with her crayons and a block of paper. I might be working my way through the pitfalls of English orthography to prepare for the Arizona state teacher certification exams.

Miro puts a short board, a sort of tray, on the arms of his chair, and has at grading a pile of bluebooks. Ceci with her no-spill cup of warm milk. Miro and I sipping on steaming mulled wine we had learned how to make from our friends in the next-door faculty apartment.

Thanksgiving Day, snow is creeping down from the mountain forests. A dozen turkeys are walking slowly down Main Street, headed for the sunny high desert of sage brush and creosote and saguaro.

No turkey for us though. Wild or caged, we'll leave them be. We'll have my sopa de queso, a deep veggie casserole, cider, a pumpkin pie.

Lori takes my hand. Ceci must be dreaming. A gurgle, it sounds like, Bonita Mamá, from her bed. We peek in, pull her door ajar, switch off the lights here in the sitting room. A log or two on the fire, three candles on the mantle, a tiny pumpkin flickering on the window sill. We sit together in the larger of the armchairs. Lori curls up on my lap.

Talking softly. Thanksgiving, remember, our years in California? Turkey Day, the war can wait, even the U.S. Navy snoops stayed quiet. No welding, no launching, just turkey that day. A good holiday, maybe the best of the year. Families coming together across the country to give thanks. Not to some saint or god or leader, just thanks. To each other, to generosity, to whatever good fortune may come to one or all. Not the weeks of hoopla you get with Christmas or Halloween or Fourth of July, the avalanches of gewgaws, the buy-buy-buy buildups. We lived in the midst of that even with a war going on.

We were just kids, excited, out shopping with the rest during free time. The commercial idol-worship here, the religious idol-worship of our Latino holidays.

These Americans, though, on occasion they do get things right, but I must be careful, must never forget Zinn's bottom-up American history, Miro's too. Be prepared for intense racism, violence, inequities, wide policy swings, their bloodiest of civil wars. On and on.

Lori turns toward the fire, a sheen on her cheek, sparkles in her raven hair. Through the web of a stray tress, I see on the mantle Lori's birthday gift to me. En Pointe, she calls it. Twists of wire, bits of welded metal, miraculously formed to become my wee ballerina. Graceful arms arching over her head, a whirl of a fanciful skirt, she twirls on a single toe.

My Lori. Teaching a shop class at the high school, turning scraps of this and that into lovely forms. A soaring eagle already sold at the Vermejo Gallery. Teaching Spanish too.

She cuddles close in my lap. Her bare arm is warm against my chest, against the tiny silver spoon, my talisman on its thong about my neck, my Iguanito. Dim in the tiny vestibule, on a shelf above the laden coat hooks, there's a faint glimmer, candlelight reflecting on the polished leather and buckle of my Luger's holster.

Old Rattler, she finds every pothole, whatever I do. And now the turn off from crumbling tarmac to dirt. She wallows through a low spot. Red mud splashes on her rattlesnake gray-green hood. Spring break for me. We are off on an adventure. Wandering the desert, exploring, and heading for a hike wherever. With spring and a bit of rain, the high desert blooms. Yellows, creams, pinks, blues. The catclaws, mesquites, chollas, hedgehogs. Hackberry butterflies busy in the mallows, marigolds, gilias, the Mormon tea. A grey turkey vulture spirals high on a thermal, sniffing for carrion. Lower, skimming above the trees, a black vulture, clued by his soaring cousin, spies the carcass, wings down for a communal feast.

We stop for a leg stretch, a look at the bees at work in the yellow flowers of a brittlebush. Lori and Ceci climb into the back seat together, story time. The adventures of Butterfly Fairy. Ceci watches every word as they leave those lovely lips.

I slip away from the butterfly fairy. Somehow detached, busy with Rattler, with thoughts, with the future.

~

Assistant Professor Ramiro Valenzuela, official by the end of this second year. Three articles, one already published, the others on the way. Chile, Argentina, Guatemala. Events as they affect the ruled, their point of view, bottom-up. Not just rulers, leaders, names, dates, big-picture outcomes, the standard top-with-little-down. Good reviews, bad reviews. Am I confusing fiction with fact, a William Faulkner or that upstart Columbian journalist Gabo Márquez, with a Clarence Haring or a William Prescott? But this perspective of mine, truthfully quite inadvertent, got me that impressive title, and I do admit to myself, that my research perforce is thus far rather spotty. My classroom performance was spotty too in the beginning, nothing like a Los Etchos high school class. Feedback is good now.

A university? Seminars with the brightest, the committed seniors, some recruited as assistants. Travel, searching church records, archives, recorded interviews. More articles, more footnotes, material for a full blown text book some day. Maybe a summer break trip to Los Etchos, interviews there, archives.

We circle north and east to a main road, wait long minutes to insert ourselves into a stream of tourist buses, campers, motor homes, cars loaded with children and gear. Grand Canyon National Park. We are directed into acres of parked vehicles, but still no sign of a canyon. Joining the crowd, we find ourselves in an enormous lodge. Restaurants, souvenirs, displays, lectures, guides herding their flocks. Through the crowds, to walls of plate glass, to glimpses of an impossible immensity. Lori touches my arm, gestures to leave, leads us back to Rattler. We must find a way to experience that wonder alone.

We had seen a sign to a horse rental outfit. Three or four saddled horses and a pony, in a corral, a wrangler on a bench rolling a cigarette, no business, just us.

A day for riding out onto the Canyon rim. Trails that dwindle, become deer tracks through the thick pines. Smells. Resins, leaf mold in the damp of the melting snow, the steam from our horses. The leathery squeaking of our saddles, Ceci's nonstop conversation with her pony, the plop and the swing of a branch where a last bit of snow has slid off, the call of an owl restless for the night. Out into parkland, single trees, sage and juniper scrub, short-grass country. We move near an antlered stag standing guard over a herd of mule deer. Ancient Supai hunting grounds. The deer, the bighorn, the wolf, the fox, the hare.

The horses are restless, perhaps a scent of cougar hangs in the air. A rustle in the scrub just ahead, a white eye circled by an impossible horn stares at us for a moment, suspended. A mountain bighorn, he leaps, he is off, bounding out onto a rocky promontory, flying into the void. A vireo's song circles in the still air.

We dismount, tie our horses to piñons with their lead ropes, walk over to the rim. To that grandeur. Distance, depth, color, shapes beyond all measure. A rock falls, an echoing as it bounces down the rock face. The bighorn is far below us, standing on a sentinel rock silhouetted against the silent distance. Earth reds, yellows, blacks fading into blue mists.

The wrangler had told us of an Indian village in a tributary canyon: West, folks, thataway, few miles, then the Grand Canyon turns southward. The Havasupai, means somethin' like people of the blue-green waters. Three thousand feet, eight miles down, there's a winding trail. The canyon widens into a kind of hanging valley. Their village. A stream runs through it, cuts through a gap in the cliffs, falls into the Colorado way below. Good people, they'll put you up for a night if yer thinkin' uh givin' it a try.

We rattle off through open country to the Supai Canyon trailhead, park by a ramshackle corrugated metal shed. There's a sign on the locked door reminding key-carrying tribal village members to carry down whatever they can from the stores within.

The trail drops down in switchbacks. Talus, red rock cliffs, winding down like a vine beyond the eye of the faint heart. I could drop a pebble on a coyote two switchbacks below. It is good to walk, my backpack like an old friend, my boots in the dust, the sweat running down. Lori has a carry-frame for Ceci when she tires of skipping down the path.

Ledges, steps worn shiny through the ages. Flowers crowd around a seep of water in the rock. Monkey flowers, the yellow columbine, anemone, a bee swinging in a sweet pea blossom. The face of the canyon sweeps out into a giant step, cut by a narrow gorge, then drops into nothing. Where creases in the earth converge into the head of the gorge, there is a patch of green, cottonwoods finding water. Darker greens above, the last pines, making way to richer growths in the thickening, warming air. White flats, reds, browns, yellows in the earth and rock, lavender distances, the enormous lid of blue from cliff to cliff. Random surfaces, brilliant colors. Imprinted in the earth, the mold of all mountains, the womb, the origin of all peoples.

The path drops into the gorge. The sky is closed out by overhanging rock faces. We wind down into the earth. A brook is born in the sand, we drink, rest in the cool. Shrubs flower about us, creepers hang from the rock walls, the air is thick with their perfume, their pollen, with the voice of the myriad bees.

On, out to another giant step. And deeper into the earth. The trees are denser, cottonwood, willows, as we leave another gorge. Wild grape, arrowweed, thickets of fern. A new voice, a freshness in the air. Through the flicker of greens, a shining river of blue. We take off our boots and wade through it. Cold, the softest sand, fish nibbling at our toes. Beyond is the echo of barking, a whinny, the rhythms of an ax. The valley of the blue waters, of the first peoples of the Earth.

Two red rock pillars stand at the entrance, hundreds of feet, slender, reaching from the orchards of flowering fruit trees to the cover of the sky. Rough, carved and crumbling by time, impossibly they stand. The twins to guard the valley, the vines that climb to the sky.

Where the stream bends to pass through the village beyond, is the first house. Small, weathered, it stands there in the curve of rushing water, a field flowering about it, apples blossoming beyond. Smoke rises from the stovepipe, a cat lies asleep on the roof. A young woman is chopping firewood. She looks up, waves at us, calls us over. She offers us an outhouse in the orchard for the night, an ancient hut of sticks and mud, a window of yellow skin, a door of a stiff black hide. Clean earth floor, three cots, a wash stand, a single chair in the sun outside.

The sun leaves the valley floor early, but for hours, in rising darkening red, it stays on the rock walls. The greens of the valley fade, take on strange colors, shadowless, another world. Sounds and smells are sharper in the moistening air. When the sun has left the rock walls too, still the sky is brilliant, white over the darkening valley, lingering, holding the swallows, welcoming the bats.

She and her husband offer us supper. A roasted rabbit, potatoes, wild strawberries, mugs of water. Soon bed time. We pull our cots near the open door, watch the swing of the stars. A coyote cries through a hole in the sky, their dog lying by us gruffs in her sleep.

In the morning we go on to the village. Unsteady government-issue frame houses, the empty schoolhouse, the headquarters house, the mission church freshly painted. Across the valley are shacks, each in the center of its mounds of refuse, its swarm of children. The whining of transistor radios, the village generator throbs in the background, the heavy air carries the smell of its exhaust.

By the village store, a dozen, two dozen, men sit in the dust out front, chewing and spitting, silent. Under their Stetsons, jeans looped under sagging bellies, they pass around a pitcher of Koolaid, hand it on to us. Inside, others talk. A dam that is coming to back up the Colorado, push a lake up to the Falls of the Blue Water. Recreation, water ski across the Canyon. A motor road down from the rim. Rumors.

We're still standing. A woman appears. Dark, gnarled, bent, a braid of white hair, a greasy hide jacket, a necklace string of claws, a long pleated skirt of faded black. She drops her bundle of sticks, sits on her heels in the dust. She looks up at us, eyes a faded gray, motions to us to sit, there, on the edge of the sagging porch. Silent, chewing slowly on . . . .

Minutes later, through the hum of the men's voices inside, she clears her throat, spits, begins abruptly, her voice crackling, no introduction.

She points. These red cliffs, they surround us, they and the gods protect us. The winter, all evils. But not all Havasupai stayed in the safety of their valley home. Once they were content, they neither knew nor wanted other worlds. But their numbers grew, it became difficult to find food enough for all. At first they merely quarreled. Then they became desperate. Famine, lack of space to live in harmony, the mounting filth of their close-packed numbers. Their Council met and decided to ask the twin princes of the tribe to find a way out, pledging that they would all would abide by their decision.

The twins planted two magic vines by the bend of the river. These vines grew high, they pushed holes in the sky, and grew on out of sight. The first twin led his people, climbing up the vines, to the unknown upper world. The second twin was to be the last to leave.

One maiden, however, would not go. She and the second twin were left alone. He could not persuade her to leave. She loved her home too well. And he could not carry her with him, the climb requiring all his strength. So he left her with child that she should not be forever alone.

She is the mother of the Havasupai. Those vines have turned into the spiraling red rock pillars reaching the sky at the entrance to our village.

Those that left our valley flourished in the upper world. Their numbers grew and divided many times. Finally there too there was no longer room. They quarreled, people against people. They invented war. But famine weakened them. They turned to stealing, the strong from the weak.

In the end, the Great Coyote saw only one solution. He brought on a flood to destroy that unhappy world. But he caused one baby girl to be sealed into a hollow log and cast out onto the flooding waters. Only she was saved.

She floated for many days. Finally her log came to rest. The waters receded. She broke out and found herself on top of San Francisco Mountain, far to the east. She foraged for food. She amused herself making dolls of clay. But in time this was not enough. She wanted human company. She turned to the sun for help. He penetrated into her womb and left her with child. She is the mother of all the other peoples of today, there in your upper world.

Our college president calls me into his office for a beer, a chat.

Are you a revisionist historian in our midst, Ramiro? An op-ed essayist? That's what your students would say. As your president, I'd say bravo, Professor Valenzuela, proud to have you with us! But as your friend, I say you have entered a mine field. You've found your way in it thus far, Ramiro, but keep your sensors out. Assert with care, with deep backup. Never rely on faith. Well, perhaps that's too judgmental, though I'm never shy about my card-carrying faithless agnosticism. Let's say never rely solely on faith. And by the way, I liked your New York Times piece. The American Empire, that's calling a spade a spade. And well placed, much less dangerous than in some academic medium.

I stammer ineptly, leave.

Coffee in the cafeteria, mid-afternoon, I'm the sole customer. Stretch my feet out, slump some, sip, a knuckle to my lips. How did I get here, this American Empire thing?

With three academic pieces behind me, I'd launched into another, the string of disastrous nineteenth century revolutions in Mexico. I dug into the cooked-up Mexican–American War. Its cynicism, its greed, its ineptitude on all sides. And I was led into tracing the momentum it gave to American expansionism, even to genocide of the original peoples.

Manifest Destiny, the Big Stick, Go West Young Man, The Less Red Indians the Better. Those were America's slogans. The warlike Fourth of July celebrations by white-skins so blind to the hypocrisy and cruelty of all-men-created-equal. The Monroe Doctrine, the Louisiana Purchase, the genocide of the native Americans, the duplicitous rape of Hawaii, Teddy Roosevelt's arrogant exceptionalism, the Spanish–American War, Cuba, Puerto Rico, Guam, Samoa, Panama, the Virgin Islands, the Banana Republics, the brutal American atrocities in the Philippines, hundreds of foreign military excursions. The Morgenthau Plan crushing what was left of Germany after World War I, resulting in World War II. The empire building of Henry Cabot Lodge, his destruction of Wilson's League of Nations dream. An empire confronting an empire in mad threats of vast, maybe total, life destruction. Antisemites, racists, extremists embedded in this culture. America at the vanguard of the world's economy, its crass output, its sociocultural influence. An empire of materialism and greed. And that profound hypocrisy. To even refer to an American Empire has been considered scandalous, un-American.

Yes, it made for a lively op-ed piece. All I really had to do was reel off some items on the endless list. Let others flesh it out for academia—for me, it's really off message.

Yet can I so easily escape the consequences? And can I take on and convincingly defend an I-am-holier-than-thou stance? Look at me, my little family, in our thirties and already catapulted near the top of the global comfort heap. The winners, and at whose expense?

Our President joins me for apple pie. I rattle on.

Look at me, while attempting to revise U.S. as well as Latin American history, this America remains for me the model, the dream. It is not just the dream of Lady Liberty . . . *your huddled masses yearning to breathe free . . . send these, the homeless tempest-tost, to me . . . the golden door.* It is a worldwide, classless dream. Opportunity, space, justice, voice, reward. That is why we came here. In those days, that was what we thought we would find.

The dark side, the light side. America the model democracy. America the world's policeman. Without her the world might well be dominated by Hitlers, Stalins, Tojos. America the generous, forgiving rebuilder of the defeated. Their Marshall Plan to rebuild the destruction that was Europe. Amnesty, democracy, wealth to Japan. America, the benefactor of the third world. The model of economic might, of industrial supremacy, of scientific and technological and artistic creativity. Of progress. America to be believed in.

An exhausting argument with myself.

The click of our mail slot, the flop of mail on the mat inside the door. Ceci drops her doll, skips over, it's just a single envelope, takes it to her Mamá.

William O. Douglas University, Washington, D.C.

What's this about? Assoc. Prof. Ramiro Valenzuela, and I was Asst. Prof. only a month ago. They must have gotten my home address, the full name with its new handle, from our college Admin. Sliced open with my pocket knife, it's two pages. The Douglas U letterhead, the Dear Professor Valenzuela, and skipping to the bottom, below a looping decorative signature, Professor Zachary Taylor, History Department. I turn the letter unread face down on my knee. Ow! The vanguard of attacking academia, which article will they start with, or the op-ed? I'd rather read no more.

Lori grabs it, reads it to me. Let me introduce . . . lecture at U Arizona week of . . . while nearby, History Faculty . . . asked me . . . could I meet with you . . . new Latin American history program . . . phone, set a date.

Ramiro, love, if that's an attack, it's most subtle.

Three weeks, waves of excitement, undertows of anxiety. Surf's up by now, three PM, will he be late? Our doorbell, those first four notes of *You Are My Sunshine*, silly, irritating usually, not now. Door opens to a dark African American, short, bald, impeccably casual-dressed, mid-forties. We both hesitate, a hint of double takes. Broad smiles, warm hands, he chuckles. Look at us! A quizzical shake of his head. A pat, a squeeze to my upper arm. Right off, it's Zachary–Ramiro.

We are on our way.

Ceci is five, a tough determined little kid, and beautiful—long waves of glowing black hair, sparkles in her dark eyes, soft and welcoming, cinnamon skin, like her Mayo mother. I check on her in the rearview mirror. She's set up Rattler's back seat as her exclusive realm. Her subjects are stuffed but ornery. Squawks and whines and squeaks, even a bar of tinkly music in response to the endless tales they are being told. We two slaves are mostly confined to quarters and humdrum duties. From time to time, one or the other of us is imported into her realm to entertain and serve her Highness.

The past unreels out the back window, though some of it follows dutifully in a U-Haul stuffed with our belongings. The admin at Douglas U told us to keep receipts. Zachary writes, Everything. Gas, motels if you're not camping, rentals, and mileage for the twenty cents per. Doug U will reimburse gladly, way cheaper for them than RR tickets and Pullman cabin and restaurant charges, the freightage, the taxis, et cetera. See you in June or July, right? You'll stay with us, plenty of room, till you find a place.

A stream in a forest of aspen, a skinny dip in a quiet pool. The tent, a campfire between flat rocks, the grill, the sooty pot. Dehydrated goodies in our aluminum gear. Toasting marshmallows, a bedtime story. Distant coyote chatter, the hollow whoo of an owl, the flashing stars. Ceci beside us in her pint-size sleeping bag, we zip ours together, embracing dreams.

East-southeast across the plains, the Rockies fading in my rearview. Rattler's back window is decorated now with pine cones, a rusty horseshoe, a stuffed rabbit in the center. Ceci bounces in her car seat to Heartbreak Hotel. Miro's driving. I drift into half-sleep. Through the veil of the bug-spotted windshield the world flows by. The highway running forever on, on to its vanishing point. The endless waves of the power lines, pole to pole. The railroad tracks always there beside us, silver rails in the sun, the rare white X to mark a crossing. A lone farmhouse shaded by cottonwoods, miles of wheat, scattered cattle grazing. Silos lonely on the horizon, looming, slipping by.

A sharp thrust, my shoulder hits against the door handle, then back against the seat. What!... Sorry, sorry, a turtle, he just kept going, his right of way. Are you okay back there, Ceci? You know what that's called, Lori, my maneuver? It's doing-a-Steinbeck. That's what Will called it, we were driving down to Phoenix, remember? His was a rabbit, not so lucky.

And we are in the Dust Bowl.

The road dips down into a river valley. Cottonwoods, two iron bridges, a substantial river, brownish. A railroad station, yellow and brown gingerbread trim, a Fred Harvey Restaurant sign, paint peeling, Closed. Eisenhower's free ways replacing the passenger trains. The end of the meal-and-souvenir stops we've read about, the shabby Indians in feathered headdress, hungry, coin can held out to us. A shuffle dance to a tired drumbeat. The Fred Harvey routine.

We pull in to a rundown motor home park on the river bank. Tent pitched, we carry cook pot and the makings of a stew over to the communal grated firepit. Our only neighbors are a couple and kids living in a rusty old yellow school bus, converted, stove pipe sticking out the roof, windows mostly covered with cardboard. Guess we're not exactly on the tourist and recreation route.

Back of the one filling station is a diner, a real one, an old restaurant car, PULLMAN, big letters in repainted gold above the windows. Breakfast, yes? Two men in overalls, CAT on their black hats, are just leaving, heading for their eighteen-wheeler flatbed loaded with a yellow CATERPILLAR bulldozer. No other diners, eight o'clock is late by farm community time. At the top of the menu is a sketch of a train, a steam locomotive, smoke making a huge cloud around *Atchison, Topeka & Santa Fe*. Coffee comes automatically. Milk for the little one, kid size orange juice and pancakes or oatmeal? Pancakes. For us, orange juice, sunnyside ups, bacon, hashbrowns crispy, super crispy.

Fading black and white photos tacked up on the walls are mostly of the Dust Bowl. The rickety farm house, drifts of dust covering the porch, mounded against the abandoned front door. Cattle carcasses half buried, Model T Ford pickups loaded with families. Worn faces, rescued items. Over the coffee maker, a framed picture in bright colors of cows grazing in a Swiss Alps meadow, a Heidi cowherd, glaciered peaks in the background.

The cook is left alone behind the counter, behind the tiered stack of pies in their plastic display case. His helper left after she had brought our breakfast. He comes over to us, a starched chef's hat blooming over his prickly red face, the coffee pot in hand.

Yes, thank you, I could do with a refill. Why don't you join us? He fills our mugs, fetches one for himself, puts his hat on Ceci's head. She's delighted, sits down with us.

A pleasantry or two, a pause, a decision. I hope you folks won't mind, but I'm curiouser and curiouser. Don't get many like y'all here, not even darkies. But you don't look to be darkies, not a bit, don't talk like them. Never hear a darky talk ejercated-like. What are . . . ?

And thus begins a rambling conversation—well, largely discourse—about wetbacks, racism, black cowboys, lynchings, electrocutions in Texas, and Elvis. Then a spirited Ceci v. Cook back-and-forth. Well, mostly forth from Ceci. Backseat driving, hats, push-over parents, comparative merits of skin color. It all ends with a refusal to accept any tip, a watch-it-out-there, life-has-lotsa-potholes, and a have-a-real-nice-day.

~

Onward, south for a bit now, into the heart of the Dust Bowl, the Panhandle country of Oklahoma and Texas. Flatter than flat, the silos march by. Occasional settlements, small towns. Harsh, utilitarian, bone-tired at day's end. The soul lies hidden in the heavy grind of work. The romance of the West is faked in a tourist's ghost town. The beauty is in the skies. The whitest of clouds floating against the brilliant blue, birds circling, a meadow lark's tumbling song.

Now, well beyond a small town, we pass a huge factory, Philips Carbon Black, a sign modest to the point of apology. Endless long low sheds, belching black smoke, soot everywhere. Sticking to the windshield, in the spinning dust-devil mini-whirlwinds dancing across the road, in the creases of weathered faces at a bus stop, cow-pasture grasses weighted with black globs from the drying dew. At a lunch stop Ceci's milk is a darkish gray.

Fields of cotton now, horizon to horizon, irrigated with these endless skeletal structures, grotesque, slowly rolling over the acres, their pumps reaching ever deeper into the aquifer. The sun reddens as it lowers from a blue sky into smudge. For hours we have seen no camp grounds, no public land, no motels. In the dusk, we pull into a side road toward an abandoned drive-in movie theater. Behind the immense sagging screen, out of sight of the highway, we pitch our tent. A glum, silent little family. We heat up soup over a can of Sterno, eerie blue tongues of flame licking the pot. Behind a nearby fence, huge phantoms, dozens in the growing dark, monstrous creatures dipping slowly down, pulling up, clanking, patiently, ever up and down, drawing up the blood of our Earth. In the distance, three enormous flames rise into the dark, their angry voices flaring in the still air. Valueless, bothersome natural gas.

Ceci asleep in the tent, we pull our doubled sleeping bags and air mattress out under the moon. A gibbous moon, wisps of cloud brushing its face. I turn to hold Lori in my arms. She turns away, snores. A trailer truck shifts down for a curve, an angry rumble, its headlights passing over the derelict structure of the drive-in screen, flickering for a moment in the dew drops in Lori's hair.

Sleepless, always the clank-clanking of the tireless monsters, the distant roar of the flames. Here, the Great Grasslands of America, the land of the bison, the Comanche, the Kiowa, Apache, the Arapaho. A land that trembled under a million hoofs, it trembles now as its bloods are sucked away.

I turn to the moon. Drifting westward, lowering, blood-orange. In Los Etchos now she'd be at her zenith, peeking through the yellow mango blossoms.

My Silver Spoon, my Iguaníto here, it lies on my heart.

My Luger sits in Rattler's glove compartment.

Eastward now, on and on. We avoid the big cities mostly, and finally, far on the horizon, is a line of purple hills. The Ozarks, higher country rising out of the Great Plains. At a crossroad is a billboard. Uncle Sam, flags and bursting fireworks, an enormous arrow pointing north, One Hour to Neosho Missouri, Center of Gravity of Our U S of A!

Not tempted, we leave the thoroughfares, find friendly winding roads into Arkansas. The hills, the valleys, rivers, lakes, lush forests of oak, hickory, sassafras, loblolly, mulberry. Meadows of flowers, mists fading in the morning sun. High above us a waterfall pours down the face of a cliff, to a pool, to white water, to the valley floor. Our road must cross this newborn river. The bridge ahead, though? It's a barn stretched out across the river, shingled roof, weathered wood siding, a barn sitting on timber trestles. A weight limit road sign announces the Bear River Covered Bridge. Why?

The road follows the far side of the widening river. Bits of fields cut out of the forest, farm houses, a small lumber mill, a side road. Canoes for Rent, All Equipment, 2 Miles. Canoes, we've read about them in our history books, remember? In novels about the northern American Indians. Let's just take a look. Would you like to, Ceci?

Ceci, I try to always use English, while Lori uses Spanish. Between Lori and me in Ceci's presence, we use a mixture. Between us when Ceci's not around we use English, correcting each other as we go. Americanizing our little family. The free and the brave.

The canoe place is at a long bend in the river. It widens here, placid as a pond. There's four or five of these boats on a wheeled rack hitched to a pickup truck. One gas pump, a store with a bit of everything, a young couple in charge.

Mudge is the name, gas? Canoes. Rookies, like a demo? No charge, Adele can keep an eye on the kid. It's real easy. Okay? Here, life jackets, paddles. I'll do the stern, one of you in the bow. Bit of a paddle, then back to give the other a go. Same routine for the stern if you're game, want to do the river. Then the two of you alone, all three? Now? Still game. Gear and grub in a waterproof, this map, two three days to the lake, phone at the boat ramp, I'll come in that rig there to get you. Simple's that. Got it? Cheap too, weekday.

Lori in the bow paddling, resting, chatting with Ceci. Ceci in the middle sitting on an extra life jacket, leaning against the rubber duffle bag. Me in the stern, getting the knack of steering. Flip of the upper wrist, a correcting slight tug at the end of each stroke. Often we just drift with the current. Ripples around stray boulders, a gentle chute where the river narrows, dropping us a foot or two. Ceci claps and cheers. Cool in the shadow of a cliff, we watch the swallows busying about their nests. Off-guard, we bump against the rock wall, push off with our paddles. Out into the afternoon sun. Lori and I, we strip to the waist. That lovely back, strong shoulders, a glimpse now and then of the most beautiful of all life's shapes.

We slip on, just us, this wondrous wilderness. Huge trees we had never seen before. We learn their names from our guide book and a pamphlet Adele had handed us. The oaks and maples, the viburnum, their creamy flowers perfuming the river banks, the black locusts, the tulip trees. The air is moist, rich with the breath of this leafy dream. We rest our paddles, silent under this sparkling canopy of green. The river takes us. Turning, slowly turning, round and round. A water waltz.

The forest opens. Parkland, single immense trees spreading over meadows sprinkled with poppy reds, iris blues. White-tailed does with their spotted fawns rest by a shading tree. A brook drops down through the grasses, through clumps of watercress, splashes over the gravelly river bank to join us.

Still just drifting, it's quite shallow here. Through crystal water, a mottling of river stones slides under us. Ceci leans over the side, points to bugs walking on the surface, fingerlings swimming upstream. There's a splash ahead and to one side. A moment later, Ceci cries Look! A duck followed by four ducklings swim under the canoe.

We pull up onto a sandy bit for lunch. A log to sit on, shade from a clump of willows. Ceci bounces off to dig a hole near the water's edge, watch it fill, the sides slide in. We're on a long sandbank that partly encloses a backwater. Deep enough for a dip if not a swim. We strip, the three of us, splash around, dry each other with the towel we remembered to bring.

There's a level grassy area toward the base of the sand spit. We pull the tent from the duffle bag, flatten it on the grass, the towel too, stretch out in the sun. Ceci making a castle of twigs. Snooze, Lori, I'll keep an eye on Ceci.

Awake again, Lori catches my eye, points down at the rumpled tent, lifts both hands to make an imaginary sloping roof. We stay here for the night. Lori in my arms.

Our home on the Rock Creek edge of Georgetown, a half hour walk to Doug U, a quarter hour trolley into the heart of the U.S. government. An old brick row house, eleven feet wide, six-by-six kitchen, living room enough for a sofa, three chairs, and a table with its leaf necessarily down. French doors onto a postage-stamp back yard overrun with ivy. Up stairs to one and a half minimal-size bedrooms, one bath, tiny steep stairs to an attic capable of being drywalled into a gabled spare room and a storage room.

They say this house was once the slave quarters of a large farmhouse, later used as a part of a slave market, the slave pens. Now, next door is a mom-and-pop fifteen foot wide basic grocery store, run by a Chinese mom-and-pop.

Water cooler talk with my admin assistant. She has no inhibitions, right to the point.

So, lovey, look at you! Blacker than me. A Mexican import, a cobbler's son, son of a Native slave. And now a tenured professor, a book on the way, a home, a family, the three of you U.S. citizens now. Horatio What's-His-Name story, you are.

Me too, 'guess, your Pokey Jackson. Pickaninny granddaughter to a Virginia cotton picker slave who died under the whip, a tobacco daddy, washer woman ma. And now I'm Admin Assistant to three professors. Nice home, family. Not bad, me and you. Rat-racing, though, to get here, must admit, still are, aren't we?

Wait, I have something for you, Professor. There's this kid, Willard, second year grad transferring here from GWU. He's good, I tell you, and he needs a job. He speaks Spanish, summa cum thesis on Mexican–American War. I sat in on his admissions interview, had a coffee with him. Exceptional, and I have seen a good lot of young folks going through here for comparison. Talk to him, grab him. Rat-pack's on your heels. Here's his file. See, told you I'd look out for you. I'm real good, too, at squeezing the budget.

In the cramped entryway to our little home, on the wall by the kitchen door is the framed push-me-pull-you drawing that Ceci did two years ago. Carefully drawn in black ink, here in a place of honor. Angel-devil, good-evil. Contrasts, conflicts, hypocrisies. Was this visual dialectic instinctive to a ten-year-old girl?

On a narrow shelf below the drawing is the day's mail, a parcel. Three shrink-wrapped copies of *Perspectives: A Bottom-Up Look at Latin American History*. I pick one up. On the back of the dust jacket is a colored photo of me.

~

Lori has set up a studio in our attic, moving on from welded statues to try her hand at lost-wax sculpting into bronze. We built a wide dormer in the roof to give her a bit more space and light. Wire and metal armatures, pots of melting amber-black beeswax, heated tools, then off to the foundry. Plaster moulds, wax burned out, bronze poured in, plaster removed. Back to our attic for the finishing touches, the patinas, the mounts. Small things. Birds, flowers, dancers, nothing big would fit up there. Then the gallery, the occasional red dot for *Sold*. She is amazing, my Lorena.

So-so cook, though.

A tray of various finger foods walks by. The usual table of drinks. The chatter, different conversations, Lori and I drawn apart by the curious, the questioning. Cultural crossovers, African Americans, Hispanic novelties? Passing gentility, but underneath, a snake pit. The power elites, the ruling class. They infest that world.

Depressing.

From the wild mountains above Los Etchos, the hidden arroyos, Arizona's high deserts, lost canyons, an elk calf in mountain wildflowers, camping on a stream bank in the Ozarks. To Washington, to the brown tidal waters of the Potomac, the endless churning.

Spring break, we must escape.

Rattler still functions. Loaded with our camping gear, her voice entertains us with new variations. South and west into the gentle Virginian countryside. Sticky air in the morning sun, mist from an early rain. Civil War country, horse country. Thoroughbreds, racers, hunters, hacks. Vast mansions, old wealth, new wealth. Quiet colonial Warrenton.

Over the Blue Ridge, down into the Shenandoah Valley. Farming country. Apple orchards, meadows of alfalfa, rail fences, forests, limestone and sandstone cliffs of Massanutten Mountain. We rent a canoe at a fishing camp on the river bank, strap it onto our roof rack.

On westward to the headwaters of the Shenandoah River's North Fork. Looking for a place to launch our canoe and leave Rattler. We find a farmhouse off a cart path at a bend in the little stream. We were led to it by the scream of a pig being slaughtered. The farmer, filthy straw hat, corncob pipe, Norman-Rockwell-perfect. He invites us into his ramshackle house for a glass of water, no one else in sight, and starts telling us Civil War stories. This area figured big in the war, he says, armies of both the North and the South bivouacked here. Stonewall Jackson camped his army here during his Valley Campaign. During lulls he'd sit on a stool pulling trout from that pool. After the battles of New Market, Cedar Creek, and Seven Bends this here brook ran red. Ghosts of the dead walk these forests, seen 'em m'self. Look, you folks just leave your buggy here, one of you hitchhike back from where you pull out. No bother.

We unload by the trout pool, launch the canoe. We are off, Lori in the bow again, Ceci in the middle sitting against our duffle of gear. The water is clear and calm here, shadows of fish on the sandy bottom. We slide along, the current picks up. Ripples, gurgles, rounded boulders emerging.

Soon it's time to look for a place to camp. We've passed three tributary brooks, widening the stream, a bit deeper. It bends to the northwest, splits around a fair-sized island. Sand and river gravel, driftwood, willow brush, a clump of low sprouts around the trunk of a dying maple, split by lightning. A Judas tree ablaze with its purple-pink blossoms. A grassy bit that survived the last flood. This is it, our islet. And it's shaded from the afternoon sun by a line of sycamores across on the west bank of the river.

Camping is a routine for us. The campfire pit with rocks pulled together. The river water boiled for drinking and cooking. The dehydrated mushroom risotto. Granny Smith apples, coffee. An evening rendition of *Oh Shenandoah* on my Hohner harmonica. We don't bother with a tent, stretch out, the three of us under a tarp against the clear-sky dew. Watching the stars slide by, lulled by the duetting of a whip-poor-will and a distant mockingbird.

In the early morning, awakened by a scraping noise, we are greeted by the staring eye of a large turtle. She's holding a yellow lady's slipper blossom in her mouth.

Breakfast, a cheery *Eddystone Light* on the harmonica. Applause. A doe and fawn poke their heads through the willows.

A lazy day on our islet, a skinny dip, basking in the sun, elaborate construction of a sticks-and-sand castle directed by Ceci. Tadpoles at play in a pool. Upstream a great blue heron fishing along the shore. Her stately march, neck and legs in rhythm.

I mutter. So much for the grandiosity of Washington, for twisted perspectives. From Lori, an exasperated lift of her eyebrows. She turns to watch a frog snoozing on a lily pad. Smiles.

Sorry, sir, President Farnsworth is chairing a board meeting, running late. Would you like me to take in a note telling him you are here?

Very good, sir. I'm sure it won't take much longer.

So. . . . A Douglas University branch in Rome. Some help from American and Italian governments, big help from an anonymous graduate. Professor Ramiro Valenzuela invited to head it up. Scheduled to open next year. An alternative for Georgetown campus students, and we'll be actively seeking students of any nationality. Four-year college level in the beginning, but planning for graduate work particularly in history and political science.

It takes a week for Lori and me to say yes.

And I have a year to learn Italian—well, that's my target—and brush up on my U.S. history.

Long talks, the three of us, long walks along the Potomac, the C & O Canal, days of wandering through monumental Washington. Or me sitting here alone, a bench in Lafayette Square, jotting down a list of random thoughts.

The Palladian White House, the colonial brick Blair House, the pseudo-Gothic monstrosity of the Executive Office Building, the neoclassical Greek temples. What does this grandeur truly mean, what are its origins, its destinies? What are its meanings for me, for my little family, for the world? Why my tiny silver spoon? Why my Luger?

Democracy, power, expansionism, success, opportunity, rule of law. Achievement. Industrial power, wealth, free education, innovation, scientific excellence, idealism, generosity. Empire, global dominance. War of Independence, Indian wars, Civil War, Spanish–American War, World War I, World War II, Korean War, and now the horrors of war in Vietnam. Dozens of military interventions in Latin America throughout most of two centuries. The Mutual Assured Destruction of the Cold War, its arms race, its bomb shelters, our children learning to huddle under their school desks.

Is it Americans' sense of self-importance, of exceptionalism, that has corrupted reality? We of Latin American roots, our histories of so many failures, is there a humility there which is lacking in our adopted country. Is a comeuppance falling due here? What of Europe, of Italy. Long histories, many achievements, many failures? A different psyche there, a different balance?

Let's go see.

I work on my Italian with Vincenzo Toccacielo, a professor at American University. We go on to study some of *Inferno*, and take a side trip into Lucretius's Latin. Vincenzo puts me in touch with an Italian colleague of his whose subject is American history. So I get myself a background in that too, while always speaking Italian. He even gives me a copy of the American history textbook they used in his Bologna Liceo. Conflicting allegiances, unctuous, condemning, clearly torn by surprising twists.

We fly back to D.C. for business and curriculum discussions, and a two week vacation to visit Los Etchos, our home.

Rattler still game, nineteen years, a baby boomer just off the remodeled Sherman tank production line. A Studebaker. Abused for ten years by a demobbed nineteen year old vet, then ten years in our gentle hands.

But. Eight thousand miles of driving? No way.

Fly to Phoenix, then Los Mochis, connecting buses pothole-rattling high into the Sierra Madre mountains. Eleven year old Ceci earphoned to *I Want to Hold Your Hand.*

Ceci darlin', remember that mountain? Your ancient Mayos' white serpientes twisting down its flank?

Silly people, Daddy, that's just what mountains do. She rolls her eyeballs, lips tight.

From potholes to cobblestones, Los Etchos. The plaza is blocked off, Sunday, of course. It's teeming with kiosks of food, handcrafts, souvenirs, a band tuning up on the bandstand, electric bumper cars circling, a rickety merry-go-round. Fish tacos and Sprites for us. Packs on our backs, we detour the crowds through side streets, past the church, on to Candelario's and Ana's row house.

Huge hugs, Ceci super shy at first. Their spare room for Lori and me, Ceci in a hammock on the loggia looking out to their veggie-orchard-flower garden on the edge of the main arroyo.

Tea, cookies on the loggia. Talk talk talk.

I, your Candelaria, I'm still that forever me who keeps a close eye on your house, Miro, Lori, yes you Ceci too. The garden, your Mango Tree. I keep the roof sealed. The renters are good people. Fear not. Los Etchos is busy, thriving. Cattle ranching, marijuana. Gringos buying up, remodeling, retiring to live in many of the abandoned mansions of the silver mining heyday. And busloads of tourists. Mexicans almost every weekend, convoys of American snowbirds, their RVs through the winter months.

We wander the streets and alleys, a visit to the church. Hats off. As we pass the altar, signing the cross, forehead, lips, heart, shoulder to shoulder. Not Ceci, she rolls her eyes, tightens her lips. The bell sounds for the evening mass, best we escape discretely with several others.

Pickups cruising for girls, radios with ranchero music full on. A five-gallon cowboy hat on every puberty-to-casket male. A parade of school children. Sombreros, Zapata bandoliers, damsels in hoop skirts and bonnets. Three horses in fancy tack of shining leather decorated with silver medallions, pom-poms. They're kicked with pointed rowels on silver spurs into occasional prances by their similarly decorated riders. A school band of drums and trumpets. Winding through town, a rubber-tired half-size train loaded with tourists, loudspeaker blasting. Once me at that wheel.

The five of us supper together in a back-street restaurant. We settle around a table in the courtyard. Distant thunder seems threatening, so we hurry with last bites, the bill, run for home as the rain begins. In the square, kiosks being dismantled into vans and trucks, plaza lights flickering and dying in the dusk.

We still have electricity here. The radio tells us that the Pacific hurricane originally headed for the eastern coast of the Sea of Cortez has now turned inland, lessening to storm category, but dropping heavy rain on towns southwest of Los Etchos. That would be the other side of our mountain. The rain increases, but there's little wind. The hurricane must have given up. Time for bed, Ceci, come in with us, you'll get rained on with your hammock in the archway of the loggia. Ours is a big bed.

Awakened, rapid bongs of the church bell, sirens, the unintelligible blast of a loudspeaker. Shouts. Diluvio! crecida! Running feet, the roar of water surging down the street, swirling from the arroyo into the garden, Candelario calling us. As I close our window, a crash of crumpling metal, breaking glass, tumbling lights of a car hurled down the street. We hear the water pouring through our door. We stand up on our bed, I lift Ceci, then help Lori up to stand on the higher chest of drawers by the bedside. Water rises to cover the mattress, water up to my knees. Ceci screams.

But it stops rising, the horrible rushing noise quiets. Voices calling, our voices. The flood quickly recedes. Candelario comes in with a flashlight. The floors, furniture, the courtyard are covered with inches, even feet of mud, of smashed objects, debris. We all struggle into what is left of our clothing, shoes and socks buried, pull open the front door through the mud. Voices, calling names, flashlights waving. And bizarrely, our street lights come on, flicker, but don't completely die.

The street had been packed, one side or the other, with parked vehicles when we hurried in from the rain. Now, no car, no truck, no motor bike, nothing, wiped clean. We get through the night by heading for higher ground, out of the mess and the mud. We knock on the door of our old house. The renters take us in, give us hot drinks by candlelight, their propane stove still functioning. The five of us spend the rest of the night in chairs, the spare room, a sofa, a hammock, bounteous blankets for our soggy shivering selves.

Morning. Sunshine, white-wing doves sing softly in Mango Tree. Maybe a welcome from Our Lady, she fades away. Golden mangoes for breakfast.

My family, my home. I pull my Iuguaníto from my sweater. A kiss.

A walk across the bridge over the still roaring flood, on to the Panteon, Flowers, these survived the flood in Ana's garden, flowers for Lori's parents, for my four parents, for Concepción and her child, for Ricardo.

In Rome's ancient ghetto, back of the central Sinagoga, are the third floor rooms of Pensione Odeon, a theater-of-song for us three? No. Basic, shabby, still saving pennies from Doug U's fixed housing allowance until the apartment they are renting for us is ready.

I curl, shiver, bare on our sweaty sheet. The sleepless silence, the close air, the stink of trash. The clatter of iron-shod Nazi boots on the stairwell below us, the shuffle of slippers, of bare feet in the hallway just outside our door.

Forty Jews dragged from our building, forty for one soldier knifed in a bar brawl, forty names with thousands of others cut now into the travertine of the new Holocaust Memorial on the Appian Way.

And a Rome in the throes of a trash collector strike, the Italian army an inept substitute. Ceci's contribution: This place stinks.

Two days later we have moved to our apartment near the Largo Argentina. We are on our bit of a terrace, looking down through potted plants on the spitting turtles of Fontana delle Tartarughe, on the via dei Funari. The narrow straight alley, blocks long, where once the ropemakers would twist their hemp, their henequen, into rope. A group of Japanese tourists obediently follow the hoisted flag of their guide on their way to Campo dei Fiori. A knife sharpener pedals his spinning grindstone, school kids in their blue smocks chatter, two pigeons flutter as they settle on our window ledge.

A concert at Teatro Argentina. The Priests' Alley up to the Panteon, dignified shops selling religious paraphernalia to bands of novitiates. Piazza Navona, its monumental stone ship and fountains. Mussolini's balcony over the Piazza Venezia echoing Duce! Duce! The Colosseo, Victor Emmanuel's Wedding Cake, the Forum, Teatro Marcello. On and on. This extraordinary melange of monuments, three thousand years.

Trattorie, families of begging gypsies, rows of goldsmith shops, flocks of starlings wheeling over the plane trees lining the Tiber, horse-drawn carriages for the tourists, traffic police in their white summer uniforms performing their elaborate ballet of signals, black limos of the ruling class. Kiosks draped with a thousand magazines, the sweet melody of a beggar's violin. He's wearing a two-cornered hat folded from newsprint with NERONE painted on it against a fiery background. Macchiato and pizza bianca in an elegant bar. The sudden silence of a baroque church. Seagulls squawking on an Egyptian obelisk. A kid on a motor scooter's rear seat grabbing at a woman's bulging handbag as they accelerate by. Posters plastered everywhere with political acronyms and self-satisfied faces.

And daily trips to the finishing touches on remodeling and infrastructure for Douglas University Rome. Some of the endowment fund had been used to buy two nondescript buildings near the Termini central train terminal. They were separated by the ruins of a third building which had been destroyed by an off-target Allied bomb. Our remodeling included turning that ruin into a small landscaped area, and tying the two buildings together to form the semblance of a small campus.

Friends come easily. We are interesting oddities, Romans are curious, open, helpful. Neighbors invite us in, a glass of wine, a coffee. Ceci and Lori have worked on their Italian too, and there's always help at hand with never a disdainful stare. Allegra and Aldo Turchiaro live above us on the top floor. We met when a pillowcase blew off their clothes line, a rope loop on a pulley strung across the alley from their window, and landed on Ceci sitting reading on our balcony. Allegra works in the Communist bookstore on Bottega Oscura. Aldo is a painter. He has made a studio in one end of the brick structure that houses the water tanks on the roof of our building. Skylight, electric heater, city water trickling behind the wall Aldo had built on the strength of a wink from Luigina, our portiera. Luigina, who heaves herself about in her slippers, opening the street door if the knocks and bangings are sufficiently insistent, muttering curses when someone leaves the door open.

Lori shows Allegra and Aldo her two small bronzes that she had managed to bring with us, some of her sketches her ideas for the future, and a portfolio she'd prepared for the Washington gallery. Aldo studies them carefully. The forms, the technique, the patina, the ideas, one or two questions.

Two days later he calls down from their balcony. Lori, put your shoes on, you too, Ceci, Ramiro. I want to take you for a walk.

Allegra joins us. A half hour walk through the heart of ancient Rome. We'd been as far as Piazza di Spagna. Now up via del Babuino, into a side street, via Margutta. A restaurant, an art gallery, a film dubbing studio. We are waved through a wide archway by a sleepy portiere. We're in a small courtyard. On each side are three sculptors' workshops. We go to the last one on the right, rattle the iron grating of the high, glassed door. We can see dim forms through thick layers of cobwebs and dust on the glass. The door rolls open on two complaining wheels. Louis Armstrong on *Blueberry Hill.* And Mike, pronounced MeeKAY by Aldo, holding out a hand splattered with black wax. Blue eyes, a mess of mousey hair, khaki shirttails over ragged jeans, sandals held on with bits of rope. Muscular build. Leathery pleasant face.

Six of us manage to fit around a metal table on the sidewalk at a gelateria down the street. Ice creams in little cups, triangles of flakey cookies stuck into the pinks and greens and chocolates. Conversations bouncing around, Italian and English. Mike, with his Italian wife Gina and son Paolo, are moving out of Rome to Bracciano, a medieval town on a cliff above a crater lake thirty–forty kilometers north.

Lori, listen in. I've a studio set up out there, going to give this one up. Like it? Aldo came over yesterday and showed me your portfolio. You're a natural. You'll want to do big stuff. Tell you, I'll keep on renting it, 1948 rent, pennies. Far as the landlord's concerned, you'll just be my apprentice, my School-of-Mike. Who'll know? Deal? Good. And I'll give you some tips on where to get the wax, and the foundries, the galleries. It's the foundries, most of them out on the Appia Nuova, that bring us here from all over. Best in the world.

We move on, seal the deal in wine, langoustines, and stories about fellow sculptors in Rome.

About the Jewish guy from Brooklyn. He too had been here since the war. He has a studio out on the Appia Antica. Several lost-wax bronzes awaiting their patina. A marble Rabbi. There's a clock on the wall with numbers in Hebrew, the hands going around counterclockwise. Aldo thought that was a joke 'till he took a trip to open a show in Tel Aviv. That's what clocks can do in Tel Aviv.

About Angelo who left Rome when he switched from bronze to marble. He'd moved to a hut in mountains above the Forte dei Marmi to be near the marble quarries. Frigid winters. One dark evening he opened his front door, stepped onto the threshold to make room for more vino. In the lamplight from inside, a fox looks up at him in the snow, shivers, slips by him. They climb in under the blankets, spend the night together.

Lori rises, steps around our table. Hugs and kisses to Mike and Aldo.

Corrado Baffigi was referred to me by a contact in the American embassy. I took him on as a consultant. He soon became my untitled but well-paid personal assistant for just about everything. A few years younger than me, he was a street kid in Naples during the war. When the Allies landed in Salerno he latched himself onto them, learned American English in a flash, became an unofficial interpreter, a kid who really knew his way around in Byzantine Naples. The angles, the centers of power, the black market, the brothels, the Mafia, the dangerous leftovers of fascism, the turncoats, the best ways to sneak through the Off Limits, the bribable MPs, where to get Cuban cigars, whiskey, how to forge a three-day pass, where the pornographic paintings are in Pompeii.

In the days of the Marshall Plan, when the head of the American Economic Aid Mission often had more power than the ambassador, that's where he really came into his own. He was brilliant in showing officers of the Aid Mission ways through the intricacies of the Italian ruling class, in finding the power points, in how to use them.

From street kid, to smart, effective, loyal aide. To become my friend.

Corrado and I are leaning into plates of spaghetti, our beer bottles dripping condensation on Birra Moretti coasters. A plain little restaurant near our campus, it has a small courtyard in back. We sit in the shade of a mimosa tree. Late summer, we're gearing up for our first term. Students are beginning to check in, directed to the host families where they will live. We lunch together often, trying, though, to not bring the office with us. And we speak only in Italian.

Ramiro, a question. Over the door on our way out to this courtyard there is a rifle. It's on a carved wooden mounting. It reminded me of a question, that I've been meaning to ask you. On the mantlepiece of your office fireplace I've noticed three objects, Lorena's bronze statue of a dancing girl, Ceci's framed drawing of her devil-angel beast, and what looks like a pistol in a leather holster, a Hakenkreuz, a swastika, engraved on the flap. You've told me about the first two, but may I ask you about the holster?

I am asked about that often, and my answers are never quite the same. Today I say: There is ammunition in the pocket on the holster and a Luger pistol inside. Why would I would keep it with me, bring it across the border into the U.S. with all the red tape involved? And now more hassle to take it here? And then to display a Nazi symbol on the mantle? Why would I do such a thing? If you have a pistol for security reasons, classically you put it in a drawer, your desk or bedside table, hidden. Perhaps for sport? But I have only fired it once.

I'll tell you the story of how I came by it another time—the U-133, Kurt, the gold, the cave in the mountain. Yes, I guess there is an element of the keepsake explanation. And ultimately it represents protection. Yet it is an evil object. Is evil necessary for protection?

Will you split another bottle of Moretti? Corrado asks me. He is curious, I can see that in the way he leans forward as I speak.

Have I ever shown you my Iguanita? Look, this silver spoon hiding here over my heart. It too is a talisman, but a reminder of origins and the miracle of life. Other stories, other times.

On to our appointment at the Ministry.

And later a Parioli cocktail party. Corrado did not warn us, being cautious. Perhaps not knowing us well enough, or even as a kind of joke. It was not the crowd that would be of much use to our newborn University, and they were not likely buyers of Lori's thoroughly unconventional sculptures.

Parioli, a glassy Babylon growth hanging in stuccoed concrete and travertine on a hill over glorious Rome, a chrome-plated answer to Mussolini's fascist art. A valet at the door ushers us into the gloved hands of the lady's maid taking wraps in the master bedroom, a mountain of minks already. On into a sea of little black dresses reaching precisely to the calf, blue regimental cravats in darker blue waistcoats, cresting here and there into the white jackets, gloves, and sparkling epaulets of the waiters passing with trays of drinks and finger food.

Haven of new riches, much of it the result of the innocent generosity of America's Marshall Plan intended to help in the reconstruction of a Europe devastated by World War II. The speculators, the functionaries, the percenters, the lawyers piled on lawyers, the diplomats uncomfortably rich, commodity dealers, nobility immigrated from the provinces, the owners and the owned, the bought and the sold. The scramblers for new position, the patchers up, the patchers over.

An obviously fashionable surgeon latches onto us, casually tells us of his specialties. Abortions, restitched virginity, and the noses, thousands of noses, an endless queue of them, bent, hooked, blossoming, flat, pugged, plugged. Turned to gold. Our hostess sweeps through the guests to ask a new arrival if she would like to be introduced. Thank you, my dear, but of course not. Such a bore. Those worth knowing I know. A tilt of her expensive head, eyebrows up, hands raised, opened slightly.

And there is the Via Veneto scene. We are just up the street from the American embassy. This time Corrado warned us that its brief dolce vita heyday was turning tawdry. Harry's Bar is still five star, but the sidewalk scene in front of the famous Doney is another matter. Paparazzi, prostitutes, girls desperately posing to catch a film producer's eye. A half-starved German tourist trying to be

Norwegian, the pickup boys from Naples, the search for assignation, whatever sex might suit, whatever role required. The Americans looking casual, embarrassed, an eye to their comforting embassy next door.

A middle aged man, rather nattily dressed, alone at the sidewalk table next to us, swings his chair around, introduces himself in an exaggerated British accent. Bleary-eyed drunk, his hand shaking, wine splashing. An awkward conversation, full of gaps. The story of his life, of his heterosexual failures, his homosexual grief, interrupted by glances of shattering jealousy half hidden by puffs of uninhaled smoke. We resort to silence in our brandy glasses. He keeps glancing up the sidewalk. A few minutes later a particularly Botticelli boy comes strolling slowly toward us, his velvet trousers clinging to his crotch, his thumbs hooked in his belt so that his fingers point down in a V. The boy stops by us as if to look across the street at a friend, his hips only a few inches from our interloper's face, his fingers moving in slight caresses.

Klieg lights come on down the street in front of the Excelsior, a film star? Via Veneto has been fancying up. Newly planted trees, huge pots of flowers here and there. Cameramen are setting up their equipment when a large magnolia tree in full flower, no one near it, no wind, teeters, falls across the street branches cracking. It has no roots, none. An MG blasting down the street swerves to avoid the tree, hits a gesticulating policeman full on. More police, an ambulance, the body on a stretcher, face covered.

Buon compleano, carissima Ceci. Sixteen years ago, under our Mango Tree. Your mama a penny-pinched secretary to our mayor, me a callow school teacher, dear Abuela, and you at your mother's breast.

Is Abuela still there, swinging in that same hammock, for us?

Here, for you, my love.

I hand her an envelope, a postcard, a brooch pinned to it. A silver paddle, two tiny diamonds. Her quizzical eyebrows, her hands raised, empty.

Pretty, thanks Papá, but?

The postcard. It looks across the narrow Ombrone River to a black cliff, a Tuscan town on the top, Civitella Paganico. We three will go there, joined by a dubious Mike and Gina, their eager son Paolo. Next week, three canoes, from near Siena to the Tyrrhenian Sea, three days and nights camping.

Clear water, fast flowing at first, mild rapids, gorges. Hills, forests, meadows. Many low weirs to portage, some seeming ancient, diverting water into irrigation, or in one case into a millstream for an abandoned mill. Camping among the willows on a sand bank, the next night on the pine needles in a bit of forest. We have one big tent, but have still preferred, all six of us, to sleep under the stars. Until the last day we see no one, not even a fisherman, yet this is Tuscany with millennia of teeming human history. Just the one town, Paganico, hundreds of feet above us, not a soul to be seen. Those first two days as if we had returned to the plague-ridden Middle Ages.

The last day, from hills into rich farming country, marshland, bullrushes. The Maremma. Farmers getting in the hay, cattle stirring up mud as they wade in to drink. The remnants of a ferry crossing abandoned when the first bridge in that stretch was built in Mussolini's time. The remains of the ferry raft, a rusted broken bit of the cable that had stretched across the river. The raft would be tied to a pulley running on the taut cable, using the flow to pull it back and forth according to the angle at which they fastened it to the cable.

As the river slows, we set to with serious paddling, hour after hour. It bypasses Grosseto, meandering in wide loops, on to the dunes and the sea. And a swim.

A plume of yellow flowers, twigs of a tamarisk silhouetted against a half moon. It sways in the night air coming from the sea, caresses a golden cheek. We stretch out on the warm sand around the embers of our campfire, the four of us. Gina and Paolo are hitchhiking up to Buonconvento to stay for the night with a cousin of Gina's, to then drive our two vehicles down to the coast to retrieve us and the canoes.

A nightingale begins with a *jug jug*, continues with series after series of his powerful liquid songs. A scops owl replies with his *kyoot kyoot*. We look out over the beach, dying waves leaving phosphorescence sparkling in the sand. Mike passes around a fiasco of red wine. Quiet conversation. In a pause, I pull out my harmonica, warm it up randomly, then try *My Old Kentucky Home*. Unreasonably, it was a popular minstrel song even in Los Etchos. I play it through twice at different rhythms and tonguing. Scattered with undisguisable mistakes. A third time, I muster my most ridiculously nostalgic mode, single notes drawn out in exaggerated tremolo. I stop for breath. I expect laughter and thunderous applause. Instead, a sob from Mike, tears reflecting the moonlight. Silence.

Mike shakes his head in disbelief, a wry smile, an apology. That song, Ramiro, it stirs up a string of memories. War, early years in Rome, visits Stateside. A mix. Nostalgia, sadness, anger, judgments, shame.

The waves on the beach, the tamarisks, that song.

I, Mike, a dogface, a buckass private, a kid in the Third U.S. Infantry Division. We've secured a beachhead on Morocco's Mediterranean coast, little resistance from Pétain's forces. A night of waiting for orders. Murmurs in the dark, the rhythm of the waves, the fireflies in the dune grass, munching K-rations, smoking. Some of us still numbed with fear. A corporal plays *My Old Kentucky Home* on his harmonica.

Days later we're ambushed by a hundred of Rommel's tanks. That corporal, a bluegrass farmer's boy, volunteered on his eighteenth birthday, like me. We did basic training together at Fort Devens. He's cut clean in two by a shell.

Years of horror.

Landing on the south coast of Sicily. Three of our platoon killed by mines. A soldier paralyzed by fear, given a vicious clout by General Patton for being a coward. Racing north and east, leapfrogging the Germans, racing for Messina. Only catnaps for three weeks. Exhausted, filthy, hungry for anything but the K-rations.

Landing at Salerno, trucked through the squalor of Naples, the cheering throngs, wine, girls. A hail of candy and cigarettes from us.

Stopped at Monte Cassino. Thousands killed, the river running red with our blood.

Another landing at Anzio. Pinned down for a month by massive German forces, eighty-eights slaughtering more hundreds of us. Desperate digging in, most living largely underground. Ten of us crowding into a concrete bunker above the beach. A bottle of Schnapps forgotten by German artillery men in a niche in the back wall.

Breaking out, liberating Rome. More throngs. Fancy MPs waving us on through. Hotels filling up with rear echelon staff even as we are trucked through the center and on north.

To rest, finally, while other armies slog on to Florence, to the Gothic Line, to freeze in the snow of the Apennines, the terror of the German artillery. We regroup, take in hundreds of replacements, supplies. A tent city, training, waiting for another landing, we'd guess. Lectures on condoms, rifle drill, hand signals on the firing line. Malaria pills. Atabrine, horrible taste, stick 'em in your shirt pocket, forget, wash the shirt in your helmet. We all have that yellow stain. Odd thing to remember.

Chow line, food slopped in your battered mess kit, a sugary pink drink in your canteen cup. Back in line for a scoop of orange jello—swarming with yellowjackets. Armed Forces Radio blaring the news, the tally of the votes in the Frank Sinatra versus Roy Acuff popularity contest. Acuff and his *Great Speckled Bird* with ninety percent. A smuggled radio picks up a Nazi broadcast. Lord Haw-Haw in BBC English telling us of massive German victories, Allied defections. *Ici Radio Monte Carlo*, announcing in German that there are no Allied bombers over the entire territory of the Reich.

Sorry, guys. Mind if I ramble on?

A loudspeaker announcement from the bridge of the LST. Alpha Beach, men, Cavalaire-sur-Mer. We shall land at oh eight hundred, disembark in order, weapons ready. Tanks, assault company on foot, troop trucks loaded, troop trucks empty, supply trucks and tankers.

We'd been on deck till oh six hundred, watched the bombings, thousands of Allied planes coming in from the southwest, the shelling from the crowd of battleships, cruisers, destroyers appearing in the dawn. Our enormous flotilla of landing craft stretching out to the east, Saint-Tropez, Saint-Raphaël. A pfc standing next to me had a road map in his pack.

Some of the ships were putting up blimps, a thousand feet or so, on steel cables. Two German dive-bombers, Stukas, come in to attack the invading fleet. One hits a blimp, the hydrogen explodes in a sheet of flame, the Stuka spins down into the sea.

We're ordered down into the landing deck of our LST, jammed with troops, trucks, a tank to lead the way. An hour, mostly silent, sweating with the heat and the familiar fear deep in your belly. Fiddling with your M1, checking the safety, adjusting pack straps. Get in line for a last leak.

Grinding onto the beach, the maw opening, the ramp down, we scramble out onto the sand, no wading this time, no enemy fire. Most elements of the division come in on shallower beaches from LCIs, wading in hip deep, M1s over their heads.

A race up the Rhone valley, leapfrogging on foot, trucks, hanging onto tanks and personnel carriers. Snipers, mines, rearguard engagements. Two killed in our company, a bullet burned a groove in my cheek. Foothills of the Alpes Maritime, and on to the Vosges. Jerry's dug in, concentrated artillery, and we are out of fuel, ammunition, food. We dig in too. Autumn cold, rotating duty on the line, and back to warmth and food in an abandoned farmhouse cellar.

Slog up to the line, the mud and snow, feet wet and cold, trench foot a worry. Feeble afternoon sun. Artillery coming in, closer, hunker down. Have they spotted us?

That's when I get my Purple Heart, piece of my thigh dug out with a bit of shrapnel from their eighty-eights. Our first lieutenant and a staff sergeant, both new to our company, come into our field hospital ward, a converted schoolhouse. They have a list and a shoe box of ribbons. They mumble patriotic nonsense to each of us, and with me they add, Corporal, you are the last of the Charley Company to have made it all the way from Morocco to here. You're in for a Silver Star too. They'll parade you in your hometown.

They pin the purple ribbon to my hospital shirt, check me off their list. Five landings, a handful of battle stars, a hole in my leg. Dead bodies, torn bodies, destruction. It is horror, not purple in my heart.

I give them a silent middle finger.

Gina and Lori climb into their sleeping bags. Mike and I finish off the wine. Come, Ramiro, check out the beach, a walk in the light of the rising moon. It has helped me to talk. I have another story to tell you. Love and remorse. Sort things out, get through the bad, find some good. Memories can be present events yet with the chance of deeper understanding. Like that Purple Heart thing. My middle finger itches right now and is glad to be ever on the alert.

So, let me pull another bit of my life into the present.

Best that Gina and Lori have hit the sack. Gina knows the outlines of the story I would tell, but I don't want to drag her through it again, that would be painful for her.

So. War's over. Art school on the GI bill. Sketching, shaping, carving, the intricacies of the lost-wax process. A Fulbright grant gets me to Italy, to wander the country-side, the museums, the churches. A backpack and a sketch pad. To Rome, to Via dei Serpenti, a loft as studio and home, high in the church bells of Santa Maria ai Monti across the street.

A studio soon filling with spindly armatures, swirling black figures looping, curling, obeying, sometimes mis-behaving. The pungent smell of beeswax heating on an electric burner, moving shadows of the pigeons on my skylight, the click-clicking of their claws.

Down the spiral of stone steps, each landing with its own door, its own pail of trash. A cat leaps from one pail, streaks away. A child climbs past me, my leg a useful handhold. Out into the alley, pressed under black medi-eval walls.

Sketching a gaunt baroque saint on the church façade, I'm sitting at a wobbly table outside a café, under a stone arcade, rain washing through the mist, steam rising from my glass of hot bitter vermouth. Lunch in a cel-lar restaurant heavy with mildew on the vaulted ceiling, with the fumes of macaroni and bean soup. Crowded, eating, arguing, bundled in scarves and coats, a variety of wooly hats. Tongues rattling with the plates, spaghetti twisting against a spoon, decanters of vino nero.

A young woman comes in from the street, closes her

umbrella, shakes it, props it in a rack, scans in the gloom for an empty place, finds me. No, it's not occupied, please do.

She murmurs thanks, unbuttons her coat but leaves it on, sits, shakes her hair loose, adjusts the generous cleavage of her dress, taps her fingers nervously on the table, looks anywhere but at me. Pretty, wan, heavy on the makeup, short black hair in bangs, cracked fingernails. A waiter in a stained apron puts a half liter carafe of red wine and a glass before her, Here's your usual, Anna.

She looks at me, green eyes that quickly slide away, asks for a cigarette, fingers tap tapping, jumpy, awkward. A novice at her job, embarrassed, even ashamed?

Anna, right? My name is Mike, will you join me with a plate of spaghetti? Thank you, signor Meekáy, yes. The conversation is slow-going at first, but gradually she relaxes, the tapping stops, the eyes steady. My passive ways, my respectfulness, the telling of bits of my story, she is clearly calmer. She begins to talk too, bits of her inevitably sad story.

Two more meetings for lunch, a friendship evolving. Her story opens up. The bombing and strafing, the German occupiers, abuse, rape, cruelty. Hunger, illness, so much death. She lived alone with her mother, one dark dank room below street level. Her mother sold mushrooms till she died of a rotten stomach a few months ago.

Would you be interested in modeling for me? Can't pay until I sell something, but we could go on lunching together. My studio's just up the street. Come.

From the rats of her cellar home to the pigeons of mine.

We are lovers. Her green eyes, her soft body, her silence, her song. Her pleasures. Sweet pea vines she grows for us in a big tomato can on the balcony over the market place. Our watermelon parties, spitting seeds into the dark beyond our candle, curses from the street. Bus trips to the sea, clam digging under the waves, learning how to swim. Wild strawberries to find in the grasses on the banks of a crater lake. Modeling for sketches, helping with the wax, tidying up. Always her wonder at the sculpting. Always there, always attentive.

Sometimes scared. My irritation, my criticisms, my moments of anger. Unreachable me, turning away. The uneasy choosing of an evening's film to see, my taste disguised as logic and truth. Afterwards, over supper, I spout elaborate explanations of the film's symbology, she so attentive, her eyes on my lips. She takes a toothpick, digs idly in her teeth. I push her hand down firmly, I put her forgotten napkin in her lap.

The books I'd give her, stared at day after day. Newspapers. The third page, culture, not the crimes. Innocent questions, my impatient answers. My announcements of her feelings, tastes. My ridicule is met by her silence.

She can lift me still with her finger tips, high above the bell towers, high among the swallows. Yes, but ours is a life with many humors, sun with many clouds.

Sometimes, searching for ideas, for new essence, new expression, the skeleton armature meaningless, the wax turning cold and hard in its pot, sometimes I watch her, my Anna, there through the forms of other statues, posing for my sketch book. I look for new meanings, new expressions. Nothing. I blame her, I goad her, I rage at her with silence or a sneer.

I make the clouds and watch their shadows.

My hands, forever sketching, molding in the wax.

I stand now by the wall at the back of the studio. Great sheets of newsprint hang there. The charcoal rolls dry in my fingers, the sun strikes the opposite wall. Statues waiting. My hands are cold with fear.

Anna, come quickly, I must catch a mood. Quickly! She comes through the statues, stands naked before me, sleepy still, not quite understanding—to make love, to pose? Her hands to her face, her arms to her wistful breasts, her hips half turned from my look.

Not bare-assed, I shout. Put on your dress. I want the pose of a streetcorner slut, a puttana.

She shrinks to the floor, kneeling, curling forward, her breasts crushed to her thighs, shaking with her sobs.

Again: Get up, your dress, now!

But she stays curled tight on the floor, keening with her sobs, pounding the floor with her fists.

I leave, enough, enough. Hopeless. I spiral down, trembling with rage . . . and fear.

A noise her scream?

Outside, the street is crowded, loud voices. I step through the open door of a church. Silent, cool, empty. I've never been in till now. Still trembling, terrified. The altar, the crucifix, incense lingering, trays of burning candles. The confessional. Pay up for forgiveness.

I have no faith.

Flowers are best for forgiveness. Nonnina with the hunched back, the tray of flowers. Violets? She asks. Yes and I pass some coins into her palm.

Winding up, the street sounds fading, the light a single zigzag, orange through the fly-specked glass. And further one slot window, dazzling sun. Here where I often stop to sit in the ledge, to look up through the slicing sounds of palm leaves, to admire the baroque curves of the lantern on the Holy Mother's dome rising against the sky. I lay the violets on the cool stone, not wanting them to suffer the heat of my hand. It is pleasant here, this nowhere, peaceful, unassailed.

The violets waiting.

Back up the spiral, slowly, decided, no half ways left, only worn stone steps turning up and out of sight. Only my door, beyond the final curve. Eleven steps still left to climb, here where I spilled hot black wax.

My statues lifting through the dusty white air into the sun. Do they teeter there, topple, burst through the door, to tumble absurdly down the stairs, crumbling ghosts that crowd past me to be dust and dirt as before?

My Anna. My hands like the cold damp stone. The violets have fallen, so hard to grasp them, to pick them up. There beyond the statues, standing by the gas stove in her flowery cotton frock. She'll be busy with her wooden spoon in the terra cotta pot. She'll start at the sound of the door closing, but she'll keep her eyes quite turned away. Waiting for some sign. Just one soft word and she'll come racing to me, her eyes full of sun, to fling herself about me, run her fingers in my beard, laughing, forgiving and forgiven.

My feet move slowly on the stairs.

My door, unpainted, sagging, scuffed at the bottom from impatient kicks. Little piles of sawdust lie on the sill. Sometimes, in the silence of the night, I can hear the ceaseless chewing of the termites. Its ring of iron, its rusty padlocked bolt, its hand-forged hinges. The ring for pulling it shut, twisted, hammer-wrought, hanging black against the gray wood. I perch the violets there, fumble with the latch.

The door swings open, I know just where she'll be. The sun has slid from the studio, the air is gray, the weight of dust. Tombstones of clay, of wax and plaster, I move through them, motionless. I know just where she'll be.

Here, in the farthest corner, her corner where she'd hung her mirror, her jars and tubes on a box, her clothes from two wooden pegs. Where she'd propped up a mattress, where she'd sit through the hours, stare through her tears at her book.

Here, stretched on the floor, her black hair staining the stone.

My wax-stained hands on her white flesh, I lift her fingers from her eyes, the palms open over her parted lips. I lift her arms from her breasts. One cut through, almost severed when her first stab had slipped on the bone. And just below the wounded breast is the handle of the knife.

Useless butchered breast.

Knife of many uses. Bought from a jangling barrow in

the morning market place. Sturdy, rostfrei, wooden handle, pierced for hanging on the wall. We'd take it with us for the clamming, to the lake to open nuts. It would cut wax blocks so neatly, slip through clay, peel dirty fruit, tighten screws. I'd pare my nails, dig out the dirt.

Many many uses.

Pull it from her flesh, does it hurt? Watch a bubble in the blood, growing, bursting, her last sigh. I close her eyes and dry her tears, fold her arms to cover her wounds. I wash my hands, wash the knife, hang it in its place. So not to see, so not to think, so not to vomit. My sheet spread out to clothe her, to hide the mess that seeps from her still. The incontinence of death.

Manacled wrists, riding off to jail. I'd screamed from the window, down the tunnel of the stairs. They come, people, police, attendants, doctors, stretcher bearers, reporters. Manacled and dragged away. People spitting, tearing at me, loud red voices crushing.

Questions questions questions while I stared at my blackened hands. Questions always circling back. The knife. Washed and hanging up, the hands rinsed. Breath bubbling through the blood. Two months of questions without answers, why the knife? I do not know. Witnesses, I started up my stairs one hour before I called. One hour watching palm trees? I do not know.

Two months and then released.

Trapped forms, lifeless, I move among them, my feet slip in the dust of the stone floor. Iron fastenings across the door, window bars, the grate across the skylight. Unmade bed, the sheets I'll burn in the stove. My hand remembers the package in my pocket, signed for, sealed, at my release. Here, I open it, crumble the red wax, carefully wrapped. They've given me back my knife.

The knife, I was trying to help her. The pain, perhaps, or a touch of my hand to give her back her life. Would it do, left dirty, we use it for peeling fruit? My hands, would they stain my statues?

The bed where I sit is lumpy and hard. Summer garbage smells curl in from the spiraling stairs. Repair shop hammerings on a battered fender. Pigeons shit on my skylight, squawk their lusts, croon stupidly back and forth, nerves pattering on the glass.

These hands, pale from jail, unaccustomedly clean, the last to touch her in life, the first to touch her in death. Hands, she'd asked for their help. That last touch, cover the bleeding from her heart. So must it be.

The moon leaves a path of gold on a still sea. We walk back toward our campsite. Mike stoops, picks up a starfish stranded on the wrinkled sand, tosses it home, out to that path to the moon.

Mike, my friend. The beauty of your work. The miracle you give to your statues. The life, the kindness you give to your family, friends. To that starfish.

Yet too that cruel destruction of your Anna. That knife, that breast. They are yours.

A story that will always be with me.

Our cruelty, our violence, our greed, our destructiveness. Thus far we conquer them not.

Next Friday our University meets, students and staff. Our fourth year celebration and review of our jobs, our lives, our hopes. It would be an honor to have you there.

# PART 3

Welcome, students, seven hundred and thirty of you, last count.

Men and women, ages twenty to fifty-one, nine countries now. I see many of our staff, faculty, friends out there too. Our fourth year of Douglas U in Rome.

I'm not much of a lecturer, more comfortable around a table or a fireplace or a picnic spread than an hour at this lectern. So . . . I invite eleven of you to come up here onto the stage, join me in this half circle of chairs. Let's say those of you sitting on the first eleven aisle seats on left side of the right aisle (your right-left not mine) of the first eleven rows, students only. Yes, you, along that aisle. Please.

Greetings. Have a seat. No, no, anywhere, I'll take the last chair. Ah, Professor Fritz, random democracy at work. Please speak from your student days, Fritz. And you, Italian? Buona sera, signorina. So . . . the other half of this circle is the seven hundred and twenty of you out there. Greetings too, and in the interests of order I ask you to let these representatives here speak for you, to respond for you to the few words I should like to start with.

Not long after my family and I moved here to Rome, my wife and I were invited to join a group of scientists, academics, political and business leaders, a group formed to discuss and research long-term global problems such as the rapid growth of the human population and our insatiable demand for limited resources. Their first meeting was in Rome. The group became known as the Club of Rome. They began working with a small group of scientists at the Massachusetts Institute of Technology. We recently met with MIT's Donella Meadows, a young biophysics researcher and systems analyst. She is the principal writer of the Club of Rome's first publication, *Limits to Growth*, due to be published this fall. We have read the manuscript. It is an extraordinary document. It picks up on the works of many scientists concerned with the long-term global threats of overpopulation and our extravagant demands on dwindling natural resources.

Growth and its limits became a widely argued topic in the nineteenth century, particularly in England. Malthus, Darwin, Wallace. By the end of the nineteenth century there was also some concern and research on the possible effects on of carbon dioxide accumulations in the atmosphere from the burning of fossil fuels. Resulting in global warming.

Two World Wars, nuclear weapons, and the Cold War somewhat diverted the attentions of scientists and policymakers from these concerns. They have reemerged in recent years. For example, the biologist Paul Ehrlich's recent book, *The Population Bomb*, is widely read and is making a substantial impression around the world.

A friend who is now a professor at Douglas U Law, when just out of law school in 1951, got a job working on the voluminous report of President Truman's Materials Policy Commission. It was a detailed analysis by some of the best minds of the day, including many scientists and specialists, of the likely continuing abuses and impending shortages of resources nationally and globally, measured against estimated population growth. They targeted 1975, three years from now, as the date of exhaustion of all resources. No doubt their projections are already off, as were those of Malthus, but the massive interest in the problem just after the huge destructions of resources in World War II, is reappearing now as the evidence of imminent catastrophic crises is ever more obvious and our abilities to make more accurate projections and predictions improve.

So . . . Doom.

For us as a species, for planet Earth before us, for the planet that is our home to us, for the planet after our extinction—doom has always been an ongoing threat and a long-term certainty in many minds and cultures. But in the last two centuries or so we have begun to seriously measure the threats, grasp rationally what heretofore was largely lore, resorts to religions, vague apocalyptic fears, and an endless preoccupation with life and death. Endgames and our roles in them are ever more convincingly evident.

For us, here this afternoon, a couple of generations of

our species, what have been among the major influences and events of our lives? From a global Great Depression to a World War, a war ended by the catastrophic destructions of two nuclear bombs, to disastrous wars in Korea and now in Vietnam. A Cold War, a world which will exist from now on under the shroud of nuclear self-destruction, of perhaps destruction by us of all life on this planet. A planet that is overflowing with an exploding population of homo sapiens. Those of us of my generation who live to be a hundred will have seen human population quadrupled. And as this exploding population is exposed to urban materialism, the demands on the planet's already stretched, depleted resources will increase exponentially.

So.

We as a species have lived for millennia with the threat of doom and the certainty of death, though a death usually tempered by unverified promises of an afterlife. We have accomplished much that is of great beauty and compassion, much with extraordinary ingenuity, but we have not learned how to live in sustainable ways and at peace. To create and enjoy beauty without the greed and cruelty that has surrounded us, at least ever since we moved out of the tribal hunter-gatherer mode.

In the years that we are to be here at this center of learning, let us use those years to learn from our troubled past, from our troubled present. Turn knowledge into wisdom, wisdom into action. Let us find paths through the horrors of doom, paths to life-affirming peace, equality, beauty. And that we can learn to accept that each path has an inevitable end.

So. Your thoughts. What might those paths be? How can we, this university, help find them, help clear the way?

All eleven join the conversation. From denial, to hopeless despair, to resigned hedonism, from pushing back on inevitability, to evolutional redesigning of homo sapiens, to technological solutions. To art, faith, religion.

Soon a series of seminars are added to our curriculum. Miro's Doom Dealers, they come to be called. Guests join us. Donella Meadows, James Hansen, James Lovelock, I hope to get Ehrlich. No doubt the glories of Rome being part of the attraction. With invaluable help from two graduate students, I begin to put together an ever shifting compilation of the many papers that students and teachers write for these seminars. And I find that my own research and attitudes begin to shift from bottom-up Latin American history to what Lori insists on calling doom-dealing.

Weeks after that first doom-talk lecture-cum-seminar, the three of us spend a weekend at Lago di Bracciano with Gina and Mike and Paolo. Ceci and Paolo, close friends by now, are on summer vacation from U Bologna. Paolo had chosen Bologna for its environmental studies, Ceci followed him.

No, it's not like that, Dad, she told me. You'd be a bit close in, your-Dad-Prez, all that, and I'm already on the Italian education track, what with four years of liceo. Bologna is right for me.

I agree and earn a kiss.

We tent on a bit of beach between Mike's new studio and their cabin. Volleyball, floating on air mattresses, fishing for pike, long siestas. Sun setting behind Castello Bracciano, fiery edges on thunderheads to the south, we roast our pike over a beach fire.

Meandering conversations, often veering into doom-talk. We toss around the hunter-gatherer premise several times—dropping the happy peasant myth, but musing over pre-agriculture human lifestyles. What was the optimum size for the community, how many hours were spent finding and bringing in food, firewood, cooking? Play, language, customs, faith? Happiness, joy?

Dear friends. Lori, Ceci, Miro. We, Gina, Paolo, and me, Mike. We are not ready yet to head for New Guinea or the Amazon Basin, to join the remnants of foraging tribes, but listen to this. Later this summer we are off to spend a couple of weeks on an island in the Aegean, Artémisos. We've been there twice. No ferry, no outsiders, no dock. We ferry to Naxos, hitchhike from there on a fishing boat, a three hour trip.

No electricity, no telephone, no motorized vehicles, no town water. Each house built flat-roofed over rain-water cisterns. No conventional doctor, no police, one mildewed Orthodox Papás, the sweat-crusted stovepipe hat, the cross-signing hand on the heart, the scraggly beard. Two hundred people, fishermen. Mullet, anchovies, bream, sole, shrimp, lobsters, turtles. Octopuses, you see them in shallow limestone caves through crystal water, stretching in the sun on coral sand. The fishing boats are made on the island or Naxos. Many still wood-pegged. Tamarask wood, pine, juniper. Mostly rowed and sailed, though one-lunger diesels are creeping in.

Plenty of rabbits, abundant figs, almonds, olives, pistachios, lemons from trees seemingly gone half wild. Two small vineyards. Sea salt scraped from dried puddles in the rocks and cliffs along the shore. Sheep and goats grazing on the one grassy hill. The wool, the milk, the cheese, the meat. Beehives here and there. Fenced vegetables behind each home.

Small plots of wheat threshed and winnowed on the threshing ground high on the windy hill. Grain ground in their windmill, the grindstone hacked out of Naxos granite, gears from olive wood. No lack of wind. Their dark bread, no added yeast, just a small bowl of mother-dough, a spoonful of honey mixed in, set aside each week to grow, warm and dry on kitchen rafters. Airborne yeast first caught from the wind maybe thousands of years ago. Bread baked each week in a communal, wood-fired oven. Whitewashed stone, dome-shaped, stub of a chimney, waist-high opening closed with a rusty tin sheet and a rock.

Not far, one might say, from your Arcadia, Pan's flute and all.

Come. See. Join us.

Fig trees, leaves dusted with red earth by meltémi winds, dark fruit of the spring harvest. Wheat stubble crackles with each step. The trail winds up into fields of asphodel, mastic bush, rosemary. From above, ahead, wistful notes float on the still air. Perhaps a cane flute, a village song, a greeting? A girl sits on stone steps leading up to a terraced plot of grape vines, tiny bunches of fruit just forming. She is barefoot, a plain skirt patched with what might be bits of sailcloth. Black hair flowing, half hiding her face, her fingers dance on her floghéra.

Higher, to an open hillside, dried grasses, asphodels outlined against a distant sea. A goat pokes in the rubble of an abandoned stone shelter. We step past a still-standing piece of its once whitewashed wall. Before us, a flashing, whirling form on a golden stage. A boy cartwheeling, calling out for joy, singing to the sun. Round and round a golden circle, naked but for khaki shorts, shining sweat, handsprings. He calls gaily to two mules circling, trotting before him, tethered side by side to a stake in the center. A leapfrog onto the rump of the outer mule, a flash of his shimmering body, he stands on the croup, knees bent to the jogging, arms spread, joyous. An exultant cry, a backward flip, he lands on his feet, running.

A golden circle of wheat stalks. A pile of sheaves to the side, two women untying them, spreading them before the threshing hooves.

As the mules circle, the tether rope fixed to the stake slowly winds up, pulling them inward, finally to stop in the center. The boy unties them from the wound-up tether, leads them off the threshing ground for a bucket of water and streams of welcome piss. Led back to the tether stake, he ties them up facing the opposite way, gives them hugs, a half a carrot, and a slap. Off they trot, unwinding, ever wider circles. Back to his handsprings and cartwheels and flying somersaults. He sings a wild and laughing song.

Chóra, the only village, white, classically Cycladic, above a small landlocked harbor approached from the sea by a narrow passage behind a promontory of red cliffs and caves. We came in the early night from Naxos, an island with a substantial town, the hub of this group of islands. In the dark, only a dim lantern lashed to our stubby mast, we saw virtually nothing. Our captain seemed to navigate by smell and sound: the echoing putt-putt of our stinking diesel one-lunger, conversation silenced.

The village was dark but for candles in a few windows. Our backpacks left in the spare room in the home of an elderly couple, they lead the six of us to an outside stair leading to a flat roof where one or both of our families are welcome to sleep. Mattresses of straw and seaweed, faded gray army blankets left by the British victors when the Italians and then the Germans had gone. There, our history, they manage to tell us. Gina had learned a bit of Greek.

We Greeks will live forever with a foreign knife in our backs.

Dawn. We wake to donkey yawns, rooster clamor, the slap-slap of someone pounding an octopus on the rocks to soften it, ready it for the grill and a squeeze of lemon. All six of us lying sleepy on the roof, the sun still hiding behind the blue dome of the church on the one street. A wind is picking up, though we are mostly protected by the low walls around the flat roof, walls to catch the rain for the cisterns under the house. The meltémi, Gina tells us, comes most summers, often daily, fierce from the north, Turkey, the Muslim infidel, another knife in Greek backs.

We crawl over to the wall, look down on the harbor. Anchors are being hauled, beached caíqui shoved into the water, some already headed out the passage for the morning's catch. Rowing, sails, some motors. Looking the other way, on a rise beyond the church, is a windmill.

The miller is setting reefed sails, the brown canvas snapping in the growing wind. Six blades, one by one he catches them, rigs them, releases them. Stately turning, creaking, grease for the wooden bearings. A boy, a sack on his shoulder, grain for the grinding stones.

Chóra, a collection of maybe thirty homes, brilliant white from the bit of bluing they add to the lime. Flat roofs, flower boxes. Basil in tin cans at every stoop or threshold, basil from the drops of Christ's blood. Chickens scuttling about, a small pig, a donkey loaded with firewood. The one kafenéion, two rusty tables on the entrance porch, blue door and window frames. They pull the tables together for the six of us. Mini cups of sweet thick coffee, their black bread, olive oil, a plate of grilled octopus bits.

The kafenéion is the only shop on Artémisos. Eggs, cigarettes, matches, a jar of hard candy, needles, pins, dusty bottles of wine and ouzo. A dented clarinet and a fiddle hanging on the wall. We buy a loaf of bread, a small round of cheese, beer, tomatoes, an onion. Our picnic, stuffed into our two rucksacks.

At the end of the village street, just before the cemetery, are the two communal ovens, whitewashed stone, dome tops, an arched entrance big enough for their small pigs. A rusty door. Firewood must be scarce. Prunings of the figs, the olive trees, dead branches from the tamarisks, the junipers, a few stunted pines, the maquis bush. The ovens are fired up once a week, ready for the islelanders' bread, their casseroles, a pig, a chicken, the occasional extra large fish.

On past a dozen or so family vegetable gardens, small fields of wheat stubble. Fig trees, higher up into the maquis. To that wheeling, singing, ever circling boy, dancing on his carpet of gold.

On to a swim in a protected cove on the far side of the island, to our picnic in the shade of a grove of tamarisks. Beyond the threshing floor we have seen one person only, a bent old man leaning on his shepherd's crook. He stopped us, handed us his crook to hold, took a floghéra from his pocket and played us a gay song, his feet shuffling dance steps in the dust.

Mike and the kids have gone off with the son of the couple that run the kafenéion, off in his caíque into a calm sea, a moonless night of fishing. Two brilliant acetylene lights off to the east, lights that they hang over the sea to lure shrimp up into their nets. Gina, Lori, and I are back at the kafenéion porch. They've grilled three red mullet for us, tomato slices, olive oil, bread, a bottle of their own retsína, heavy with juniper resin. Indoors, twenty or so men, only men, have pushed their tables around an ancient portable radio. Shouts and groans and cursing gestures. It must be a soccer game. An older man breaks away in disgust, takes the clarinet off the wall, comes out here onto the terrace. He looks at us, raises the clarinet toward his mouth.

Italiani? Permesso, cansone?

Certo, suona pure. Several islanders know and are ready with some Italian from their friendly, benevolent early occupiers in World War II. Not so with the later hyper-harsh, disciplined Germans, their brutish language.

A sad song, a longing song. Lost love perhaps? The sliding notes I had heard in a Greek restaurant in

Washington, slithering from drawn-out note to note, like a finger sliding on a fiddle string. A young woman comes up the porch steps from the cobbled street, leans against the railing, begins to sing quietly. Soon her eyes are shut, her cheeks are shining with tears.

Ten days, two weeks, we begin to learn something of these islanders, their dark sides, their joys, their hardships, their longings. Bits of Italian, English, Gina's Greek. Hours every day at the kafenéion. The owner, Manolo, had spent several years as a deckhand on an Italian freighter with a largely Italian crew. He sits with us often, though his little shop-bar-café is the hub of Chóra. Mostly women during the day, men in the evenings. Reports of their days on land and sea, gossip, laments, endless issues of failing bodies, illness. A hard life, pain, hunger, brutal accidents, death. The weather, the withering sun, the hateful violence of the meltémi wind out of evil Turkey, the dank cold of winter, the droughts and torrents, the blasts of thunder, the terror of a lightning bolt that shattered the bell tower last year.

Evenings inside. The smoky murk, the heat and hiss of two turpentine mantle lanterns. Shouted declarations, fierce hand slaps on a tabletop. Noisy backgammon when the radio has run through their battery supply.

The many celebrations. We are there for the Saint's Day. The village square, cobblestoned, between the kafé and the church. Dancing in the moonlight, hand-to-hand, circling the ancient plane tree, twirling, squatting, weaving. The handkerchief dances. A bouzouki, a fiddle, that clarinet. Ouzo, retsina wine, children everywhere mimicking the elders.

Lunchtime. We are sitting in front of the kafé, three tables shaded by a limb of the plane tree and a roofing of cane stalks on a rickety wooden frame. Antónios, smiling, cheery, Down's syndrome. He shuffles into the square carrying a small cloth bag. Salt, we're told. He greets us, everyone. A woman, her head covered against the sun, leading a donkey loaded with firewood for the communal ovens—she catches his eye, smiles, a slight bow of obeisance. Two men carrying bundles of fish nets, headed for the beach where they'll stretch them out, knot in repairs. Smiles, slight nods of respect. Manolo tells us that those thus afflicted, those stricken by Artemis, goddess of the moon, are held to be especially blessed. They are generously cared for, the last to go hungry.

He tells us that the island has held off the several attempts by the Athens and Naxos bureaucracies to install a force of three policemen. The island's way of keeping order and dealing with infringers is exile, decreed by discussion over the communal laundering on beach edge or in tubs under the plane tree in the rains when the cisterns are full, and by murmurs and grunts over the backgammon boards. Enforcement is societal.

By tradition, marriages usually occur between islands rather than within. Inbreeding avoided. Greek Orthodoxy here appears to be a mix of casual acceptance and energetic and usually celebratory events. Not the dour bitterness of the Protestants. The priest is a family person like everyone else. One crosses oneself right shoulder to left, the heart side, not like the heartless Romans. There's little of the solemn. When church fills for events such as Easter, a wedding, a funeral, the crowd is happily unruly, moving about, talking, maybe laughing, mixing throughout the ceremonies.

For generations, many of the young men have gone to sea for some years, have seen other worlds and ways. Like as not they return. Home is where they choose to marry, to have children, to grow old, to die. Every now and then a fancy yacht stops by, fancy folk row ashore, then leave. Magazines, pictures, no TV yet. Maybe a once-in-a-lifetime trip to relatives on Naxos, even Athens. There's an awareness of alternatives, sometimes even realistic options, but the people of Artémisos continue as a stable population, living much as they have for millennia.

As Gina puts it, a tribe. Hunting in the seas, gathering the products of their land with but light resort to agriculture. Powered by the winds, watered by the rains. Shunning dogma, enjoying ritual and tradition, self-governing. Ready to dance, to sing, to feast, to love. To quarrel, to hunger, to suffer. To stay, to die.

Lori, my love, look. No, you better sit down. This just came in the mail.

Yes, a Brewster Award, oh my god, a hundred thousand dollars a year for five years. Careful, your sweet eyes look to be about to pop. Your fingers to the lips, don't bite. But you're laughing? Where are you going? Not a kiss, not a hug? Champagne, it was waiting in the fridge, caviar? You knew, they phoned here while I'm slaving at the office?

Why me? My books, I suppose, the lectures, those speaking gigs, kudos for Doug U Roma, maybe my skin color, my beautiful wife and daughter? My friendship with Howard Zinn? I'd see him often at historians' conferences, lectures, speaking tours. My model bottom-upper.

Whatever the why—an adolescent Ceci would drive me nuts with her *whatevers*—here it is, a hundred thousand dollars a year for five years. With this and the build up of my TIA-CREFF fund, do we see new chapters opening up in our lives?

Doug U, it is a remarkable success, here and in D.C. Strong faculties, emphasis on teaching at the college level, research secondary until post grad. Students strong, mixed, eclectic. But maybe we're getting a bit stodgy. Infighting inevitable but tiring, sucking energy from our work. The world around us is not happy. Deep wounds from the Vietnam War, the madness of the Cold War, the never-ending arms race, the Soviet Union making moves on Afghanistan. The threat of global warming. Greed, consumerism, the population explosion, pollution, urbanism. How might we, you and I, respond to these crises? More directly, personally, honestly, heartfully? Doing, not just teaching others to do.

Is it time to move on? Lori asks. I'm getting used to Ceci being gone. Now she's Cecilia Valenzuela-Varga, she and Paolo with their infant Alessa, settled in Washington. Ceci a journalist, Paolo with dual citizenship, a lawyer with Conservancy Without Borders.

Move on? Where, how? Lorio-love, thoughts?

Well. First, a toast to whatever. Lucky you're teasable, Mister President. Whatever our next chapter may be, you and I. Eighteen years it's been. You've done your job here. Doug U Rome is in place. I'm already moving away from lost-wax bronze to small things, wood and stone. They offer a more direct satisfaction, not so cumbersome, not tied to a series of interim steps, the plaster molding and the casting being quite out of my hands. And lost-wax sculpting needs a large, permanent, equipped studio. I'm all for leaving Rome, even the best of cities can be wearying.

Lori continues: You, mi Ramiro, need a prolonged rest, I can see it, we all can. As a starter, maybe a rural setting, quiet, reading, writing, perhaps finding our ways through doom to hope. From cruelty to kindness. Enjoying little things, you and me, being close to each other.

She takes my hand.

A dove's plaintive voice, faint ring of our village church upwind perhaps two miles, Valiagli. Murmur of the brook in the borro below that ran blood red in the Siena-Florence wars. A scraping and grunting nearby. Quietly, I put down my book and note pad, climb out of my hammock, step over to the waist-high wall enclosing our loggia. He's here, almost at my feet, our immense cinghiale friend, black-brown, pawing in the weeds, hoofs, tusks, munching on a clump of wild onion for an appetizer.

Long afternoon shadows reach down to the brook. Shadows of our medlar tree, of the abandoned olives, the posts of the little vineyard succumbing to weeds. On the other side, the forest of pine, oak, chestnut, hundreds of acres, rises steeply, upstream and downstream, up to far hills, to a fortified abbey with its bell tower. Only one other structure in all this panorama. A half mile or so downstream, a stone bridge, a mill house and mill pond, the mill wheel long gone.

I thank you, my dear Lori, that we are here. A year's rent, renewable. This ancient stone farmhouse, Etruscan traces in the foundations, they say. That long drive up from Rome. Rattler Two, a well-used, loyal Fiat 500. To Siena, then a country road to Valiagli, a dirt road past a lone church in a forest, an unlikely palm tree in its courtyard. Down a forest cart path lined with head-high, white-flowering heather. Out onto this abandoned farm, this re-done ancient house, a home waiting for us.

On top of the pile of books on the floor by my hammock is Ram Dass's *Be Here Now*. As I stand under the arch of this loggia, looking out over this scene, the buzz in my head calms. To-do lists, worries, regrets for the past, hopes and fears for the future. They fade into the peace that surrounds us.

These books. Theodore Roszak, Ken Kesey, William Irwin Thompson, Paul Ehrlich, Jack Kerouac, Thoreau, Meadows, Muir, Timothy Leary, Aldous Huxley, Castañeda, Steven Gaskin, Abbie Hoffman, E. F. Schumacher, Fritz Perls, Alan Watts, David Sanger, Stewart Brand, Alan Ginsberg. And a few of the Ayn Rand types as counterpoints. I have kept Oxford's Blackwell busy with my mail orders. A chronicling of socioeconomic changes, cultural stirrings, rebellions, particularly in my adopted country. Voices of a counterculture emerging against the background of failed wars, assassinations, the trampling on civil rights, the oligarchies, the greed and corruption, the blunting of socialism, the population explosion. A different way of living. Self-sustaining, communal, renewable, living in the here and now. Artémisos gave us a glimpse of a community at least partially, though largely not intentionally, meeting such criteria.

I have not been a participant in this counterculture, merely an interested outsider. Well, perhaps connected to it as an upside-down historian in a liberal academic environment, as an increasingly alarmed doomsayer, but as a sayer, not a doer. Talk, no real walk.

Yes, you're right, we are hypocrites, says Lori. Who is not? Look at you, Ramiro Valenzuela, you have climbed out of poverty, you have confronted bigotry and racism, you have upended Latin American history, you have headed up significant new dimensions of truthful education, you have invigorated concerns about limits to growth, you have fathered a daughter who is destined to be an effective woman—wife, mother, investigative journalist.

You have enabled me to be a rather good artist as well as an exceptional woman-wife-mother. And by the way, look at us, mid-fifties, not a single silver thread in our shiny black hair. And yes, still hypocrites.

So, Lori, what's next then? Our species seems to be headed toward ever-greater nastiness, even widespread self-immolation, the survivors clueless. Can we try to walk our talk? There are ways. Have you read into any of this pile of books that has infected our Tuscan home?

Some, yes, Miro. Here and there, usually over a glass of vino nero. And have you noticed I've become a hard-working gardener? And the maker of beautiful olive-wood forms for the pacification of mankind? And yes, our year here is almost over, let's walk together, a new path. Let's work out how and where, get at it. And make it fun.

By the way, apropos a new path, I've just been reading about the New Age gathering in Vancouver next week. It looks good, I think we should go. Just don't tell the

Brewster prize committee. We have a lot to learn as we approach the last weeks of our Tuscan year.

Vancouver. Mountains above the river mouth, sun setting behind snow-capped peaks across the Georgia Strait, beaches, an island is a part of the downtown. Our Youth Hostel, noisy, of course, but quite okay. Communal bunk beds and washrooms.

IHOP waffles again, Lori?

A bus ride, and we're in this huge ballroom, our tickets punched three times now, thousands of us. Speakers' platform with chairs for emcee, sidekicks. Posters, mostly butcher paper, stuck up on all the walls. Many of the authors, funders, leaders, I've been studying in our Tuscan hideaway are on the mimeographed program. Rolling Thunder, Spangler, Caddy, Thompson, Ram Das, Ehrlich, Rajneesh, Gaskin. Several each day. Eileen Caddy has just finished describing Findhorn in Scotland, one of the best-known intentional spiritual communities, communes, really, though that word is never heard. An intermission, we pull sandwiches and canteens from our knapsacks, chat with three neighbors.

Much of the intensity in the speakers' presentations, and in this massive audience, seems to come from a wide-ranging yearning to find a way of life that moves away from violence, greed, cruelty, competitiveness, ravaging consumerism, inequality, indignity, and the growing evidence of catastrophe from global warming. A way of life that finds communal and to some degree spiritual ways to live lightly on the land in small self-sustaining communities. And the background to this yearning is a constant drumming of spiritual equality and commonality as essential to the survival of our species. Otherwise we are doomed by our rapacity.

Many paths to these goals are shown to us. Different governances, different ideas of spirituality, different economies. If you listen carefully, particularly to the spontaneous conversations among the audience, there are failures, whatever the paths. Be aware. Skepticism is essential. There is fakery, there are charlatans along many of these paths. There are woo-woo crazies out there.

Our species is a volatile mix of compassion and hate, of beauty and the ugly, generosity and greed, communality and selfish destructive power-hunger. Governance the solution, governance the problem.

Gina and Mike phoned us an hour or so ago, just after you left for the Valiagli grocers.

I told them about the Vancouver event.

They're just back from Artémisos. Turned out to be lucky we didn't join them this year. The island has lost its soul.

A ferry now, daily, straight from Piraeus. A concrete pier, hordes of summer tourists. Several cars, useless. Police. The windmill with a gross DISCO painted white on three sides. Tacky hotels, roofs spiked with rebar waiting for a third story. Several fishing boats converted, awnings rigged over banks of new seats. The tourist trade seeking new beaches.

A concrete pier, propeller thrashing, hawsers thrown to boys vying to catch a hawser loop, drop it onto a bollard. Swarms of children calling out, waving for attention, holding up signs naming hotels, three of them there on the beach at the head of the harbor, another being built. Three cars, but there's nowhere to go! And a policeman? Our rooftop bedroom of nine years ago is cluttered with antennae. The house is a police station, the couple have moved to the cemetery. Our hotel rooms are dank from new concrete.

We wander. The kafenéion, newly whitewashed, glossy blue door and shutters. We step up onto the terrace. Two boys walk past, deafened by their Walkmans. We move inside. Four ouzos, Mohair Sam on a boombox, Elvis. A bouzoúki hangs on the wall, two broken strings curled back onto the bridge. A clarinet propped on a shelf, no mouthpiece. Out into the sunset, gulls settling onto their perches, their cliff-face nooks. Past a new cinderblock structure as it belched exhaust, the island's generator coming on. One cracked clang of the church bell hanging on its gallows of timbers in the forlorn bit of churchyard. Vespers, no takers.

Flaccid food, harsh retsina, futbol on the telly. Anxious Romanians under the greedy thumbs of once-upon-a-time hardworking fisherfolk, forever squabbling in their office, grumping behind the bar, insulting the neighboring competition.

All this wrought by a daily ferry.

Early morning, roosters answering the matins bell. Long shadows of sunrise stretch up our path. Fig ovens, stubby stone, domed tops, open mouths, only one still whitewashed. A breath of juniper smoke, closed with a sheet of iron propped with a rock. They'll string the dried fruit together on a twine of grass—a confection for the last household to hold out against the onslaught of new candy.

Up into still air, into the song of a floghéra soothing a flock of uneasy sheep as they stream out of their corral. On to the threshing ground. The fading vision of that boy, his joyous cartwheeling, his song. Asphodels growing in the cracks of the limestone circle, waving their stalks of white blossoms as the morning winds begin. Khería, candles for the dead.

Is it better, Lori, that we move to Florida, build a swimming pool with that Brewster Award. Float around on an air mattress, martini sheltered in a cute umberella?

Is it better that we just fade away, withered laurels on our balding pates?

No, no. Sorry, you're my co-conspirator, we know that, Lorena. It's really not you I'm talking to, my love. I'm dealing with Brewster twitching in his grave.

Yes, Valenzuela, I am twitching. You late middle-aged emeritus researching how to become a hippy? Or is it a flower child? And did you forget that I got you into Who's Who? No, yours is not the plan I had for you, Valenzuela.

Okay, old man. Not to argue. Your Foundation requires an annual summary report on plans for and use of the award, but with no limits other than illegal activity. Our plan is simple. We fly to Washington to bid farewell to Douglas University, hang out with Ceci and family, buy a pickup truck with a camper on the back, and continue the search. Alright, call it utopian fantasy if you will, but you'd still prefer me in a swimming pool, Mr. Brewster?

A hoverfly settles on a blade of grass, stretches its wings, folds them back against its body, camouflaged as a stinger in yellow and black stripes, two wings, not the four of bees and wasps. It hops off, hovers over a pink-white blossom no bigger than its black head, reaching for a speck of pollen, a droplet of nectar. Two blossoms on each swaying stalk, the twinflower, evergreen leaves, ground-hugging in mats of runners. It thrives in northern latitudes, circumpolar. So of course, that will be the name of our community, Twinflower Farm.

Ceci's Paolo and I are sitting on a ledge over Mugwump Lake, working over the papers establishing the Twinflower Farm as a land trust. Paolo's lawyer experience he insists is pro bono.

This half section of forest and meadows, lake front, old farm buildings, with cattle and horses and chickens and bees, vegetable gardens, orchard. With Eagle Bluff's rocky peak looking down on it all.

The detailed covenants on its use and occupancy. The mission statement of our community of land stewards.

Stewardship to us occupants, ownership in Canada Conservancy. Our leadership rotating by three-year elections. A Bill of Rights in a few words.

Yes, a leap of faith for a well-established sculptress, and a retired history professor. And you're right, Brewster, with Lori and me late middle aged and dark skinned won't make it any easier out here in the boonies with the local folks. Farmers, loggers, fishermen, Klahoose First Nation. And it's quite true that we are essentially none the wiser, despite our research into the counter culture, our many leisurely visits to intentional communities over the last two years, how to create, govern, run one for the long haul, socially, spiritually, economically.... Yet I, Lori too, she says, remain convinced that our species will not survive for much longer, that it will kill itself off one way or another, if it doesn't reorganize itself into smaller, more self-sufficient social groupings under democratic benign leadership.

Greed, Power, Corruption, Denial, Technology—they'll do us in, unless....

But let's get on with it, Paolo. We've already raised most of the funds to buy the land, give ownership to Canada Conservancy. There will be no private ownership of land or buildings. The only private ownership will be of personally acquired household items. Eagle Bluff and a virgin forest at the end of the lake will be left as wilderness, untouchable. Additional construction is restricted to a limited area set well back from the lake. Within these limits, the occupants of the land will be self-governed.

Lawyer talk, paper talk, sending us on our unlikely way.

Lining up for our first Thanksgiving greeting card photo. Starting with Lori, Paolo, Ceci, me, four adults and three young children from the suddenly evicted Frazier River community. We'd met them at the Vancouver event.

We meet in the hayloft of the cow barn. Some sitting on pillows, cushions, a convenient dog bed. Others in lotus positions on counterculture prayer rugs. An arthritic on a modest chair. At the center of our circle, a crystal bowl of lake water, three bits of twinflower floating in a triangle around an island of a mossy rock. Eyes closed, silence, seeking to quiet egos, competition, noisy brains, to find some vision or voice to help answer the question of today. Which is . . .

Rory, his wife Leah, their young daughter Kendra. Join us? maybe? The latest in the dozen or so who have turned up in this month asking to join our community. She a gentle Canadian sheltering her shy nine-year-old, her husband a powerful barrel of a charismatic American. He'd been the guru leader of a commune on an uninhabited island further north, chased off by the Mounties for squatting on Crown land. Maybe it was a clash of personality, of ideology? Their record with the Mounties? We want their valuable experience of communal survival in wilderness.

Twenty minutes of meditation. A gentle ding—our Ringer for the day taps the bowl with her wedding ring. We go around the circle.

*Our Ringer Lady first:* A warm spring sun, radishes sprouting.

*The next two with similar experiences:* Friendly cows, chickens.

*Mooie:* The feel good aura of mother/child, not the father Rory.

*Linda:* A nothing, sorry, it just didn't work for me today.

*Will:* A clear voice repeating two words, Compassion and Caution.

*It comes around to me last:* Sorry, no inner voice or vision this time, just my busy brain wondering about the cult thing. A consensus, Madame Ringer?

*Our Ringer:* Near enough. Yes, invite them in for a one month trial.

*My noisy brain again, this time sotto voce:* Will telling anyone to leave be that easy? How many meetings would that take? How much damage?

A midnight phone call from a friend in Vancouver. The Mounties are on their way to Twinflower, chasing Rory, tipped off that they may be here. Vietnam war draft dodger? They don't know. I climb down from our loft, dash over to their digs. By morning they are gone.

Two weeks later, Ron, a Frazier River member of our community tells me he would like to show me something. He leads me deep into a forest of alders and salal at the far end of the lake. To an abandoned shelter, a tarp over a frame of two-by-fours. He had befriended Rory, toyed with becoming an acolyte, intrigued by the cult's reliance on God's Yes or No. He had helped the family disappear that night, helped them set up this shelter, brought them food and water secretly. Until one afternoon they had gone.

In our next meeting he tells us that Rory was on the FBI wanted list for counterfeiting, vandalism, and various etceteras back in the States, a leader of a group of left-wing terrorists, out to disrupt the nuclear weapons industry.

Quixotic again? Worthier than windmills?

Milking, bottling, delivering it up and down the island in our rusty truck. Feeding the chickens, hay for the horses and Monty the bull, checking the bee hives. To the lakeside vegetable garden for the last of the corn, twenty or so ears plucked, bagged, slung over a shoulder. A scarecrow to put into hibernation.

Over to our new root cellar, our first and highest priority project—keep us fed through our first winter. Half dug into a hillside concrete barrel vault covered with grassy sod, eight large bins built with two by fours, double insulated door, two heavy-duty padlocks now. Onions, early potatoes into the bins. Then apples.

Back of the old homesteaded farmhouse, firewood to be split for the communal stove. Into the kitchen, kneading the dough, checking on the yogurt batch, Monopoly on the kitchen table. And yet another meeting tonight.

Twinflower turns forty. Some of us originals are still alive, still here. Our totals are now at twenty-three adults and eight children.

I've never missed my summer solstice on Eagle Bluff. Two walking sticks, breathless, wobbly knees. It's still well worth it. A few hours, a meditative nap. Lori to join me later. To sleep here through the night.

A handspan or so from the tip of my nose, just beyond my pillow of moss, a red speck of a spider mite climbs a gray-green bit of caribou lichen. A miniature antler branch, it stirs in my breath, the mite pauses on her swaying perch, then struggles on to the tip. She surveys her tangled landscape, perhaps dazzled by the glitter of a mica flake in the granite ledge that is the lichen's purchase. I rise up onto one elbow, still sleepy, keeping an eye on my dot of a friend. She ignores me—a distant background, benign, not the curl of a lizard's tongue. I watch her as she turns on that antler tip, turns in little jerks, completely around, twice.

A crack in the ledge is home for the creeping stems of

a twinflower. Two tiny pale pink flowers stir in the afternoon sun, fringed tutus dancing in the rising air, their shadows twirling on a carpet of green.

Look up, up through the leaves and blackberries of the ground-hugging salal, dwarfed by the exposure, the thin soil here. Look up through the tips of the cedars that have found foothold on a ledge of the Bluff's cliff face below. The sun lingers over the ocean at the end of its sparkling path, at the greening edge of the sky.

Far to the south, beyond our island, echoing faintly against the cliffs and mountains of the mainland coast—a sonorous multitude of sound still barely in one's consciousness. A growing chorus, the gabbling of geese coming north. Their V formation appears in the blue between mountain peaks, then silhouetted against a snow field. Perhaps fifty of them. They sweep toward us, compact lines, their wings in graceful dance. I turn as they pass behind me, gliding, descending toward our Mugwump Lake. Silent now, perhaps startled by the raucous greetings from our own flock feeding in the lakeside pasture. Our flock, it had stayed through the winter, first time this far north, they say. The newcomers splash down on the lake, erasing from still waters the images of sky and snow peaks and cedars.

Here to retrieve myself from the unforgiving tasks of communal subsistence farming. Here to dream. Me, this withered, dark-skinned, displaced Mexican from Los Etchos, an explorer of doom, a seeker of tribal sustainability, a communitarian farmer. To this relic. Exhausted from what once was a half-hour jaunt from our cabin home to the top of Eagle Bluff.

Slow steps, a rustling in the heather, twigs snapping, heavy breathing in the stillness. Lori, laboring up to join me. I struggle to rise. This ancient body, weakening, stiff, the buckling joints. Silent hugs, smiling eyes, a caressed cheek. She unpacks a bag stuffed with another blanket. Mine was damp from the dew, I'd spread it on a thimbleberry bush. Two ground sheets, water bottles, food. Dried fruit, nuts, carrots, a filet of smoked lake trout. We spread a ground sheet on a patch of deep moss, stretch out in the rising sun, lying face to face. A day, two days of rest.

Morning, pink bits of cloud through the tree tops, floating in the dawn-green sky. A bell, distant, irregular, sometimes just a touch of sound, a bell buoy in the quiet sea. I roll toward my Lori, reach for her cheek, soft, smooth, her black curls.

Late afternoon, cow bells, our free-ranging Herefords amble down the dirt road far below us, across a meadow, heading for their evening milking in the barn. Monty snorts at his passing harem, clatters against his paddock fence. A mile away, yet we name them, one by one. Alternating, first Lori, then me, as they go through the open gate into the barnyard. Old friends through the years.

We have a surplus, said Lori. Perched here in the sun, munching, talking.

Have we earned this, Ramiro, sitting here, just watching, being, waiting? I overheard talk at dinner last evening, you were already up here. News coming in of the droughts to the south, of an exodus, a diaspora moving north. Are they headed here, to our utopia? Made me think. Remember the bomb shelter hysteria at the height of the Cold War? The arguments, you and me shocking our friends in D.C., declaring that to build your family a bomb shelter means you are ready to kill? Kill neighbors, friends, even family when there's no more space or provisions?

I answer: What if…? The diaspora arrives, hungry, desperate. We hide, we defend, we kill, the survival instinct? Or we all die together? Or we see it coming, we move north, more isolated, ever on the run, hoping that the growing heat of the planet, the hardships, disease, will kill them before they get to us?

You're troubled, old man, I know the look. Here, lie by me, atop our blankets, this ground sheet over us. The stars are lighting up, the aurora flickers back of the mountains, whites, greens, pale reds.

Here. I brought our pot pipes, a bag of weed, a box of kitchen matches. Light up, Miro, with the stars, with the northern lights.

Dream in these scrawny old arms, my love.

I, Ramiro, stand tall, here on the peak of Eagle Bluff. Lori sleeps on our bed of furry moss. Her hair shimmers black in the early sun. A hummingbird hovers over her, lands on her outstreched hand. As I turn to face the dawn, my ponytail slips over my shoulder. No, no wisps of white in the thick black.

I dream?

Close to our cliffs, a whale slaps the sea. Far off, Totem Inlet reaches into dark mountains, their glaciers gone for many years. The sun blood-red in the smoke of endless forest fires. On the sanguine sea, two fishing boats, brown sails limp, oars out, struggling against a flood tide. Motors discarded, no fuel for years. Together, perhaps twenty people.

I take Lori's hand. Come, my love, quick, alert the others. We run, we leap, no, we float over the path. In an instant we are there. It's breakfast time. Dangerous days, we gather now for meetings and meals in our emergency cave. We step through half-open steel doors. A meager fire, bacon sizzling on a twisted bedspring, flaring bits of grease. A battered coffeepot passed for refills.

We report to our Colony Leader JR, Ceci Jr, my great-granddaughter. She gestures for silence. Attack likely, probably tonight. She names two of us to scout the situation, calls out the day shift and night shift rosters, guard duty on cave and cabins, root cellar, gardens, livestock, periphery sentry duty, man-trap duty.

Check your guns, ammo. Your's too, Ramiro. No lights, no smoking. Silence.

And her reminder. Respect lives, yes, but survival is our final measure. Remember, we are no longer that consensus Farm, we are a Colony. You chose me to lead us seven years ago. We are each an element of one organic whole. Bees, ants, a colony. With guns—however much we would wish otherwise. Those that differ must leave.

Alert through the day, our scouts report nothing seen or heard. Our supper in the cave. Most will sleep there too. Beds of leaves, fir branches, ragged blankets, skins. Some of us are still braving the cabins of the one-time Farm.

Pale light of a northern summer night. Cautious steps, Lori at my side. We lock ourselves into the cabin we rebuilt, how many years ago? Shuttering barred windows, we light our feeble lamp, solar powered. Pump well water into mugs, ease onto our chairs by our wobbly table. Shadows of our hands on the scarred wood, ageless faces in the gloom.

Voices of the past, of the darkening present.

Sobs. A trembling hand, a mug rattling on the table top. Storied wood gouged, initialed, stained. Eyes lost in shadow. Silent thoughts.

Our dream, our bitter hope. Our home, our community, once our Twinflower Farm, now our Twinflower Colony. This once wild island off Canada's west coast. Thirty seven, I count. Families, friends. Generations. A peaceful experiment, a simple response to a destructive world.

An ever hotter world. The droughts, the floods, the fires, the storms. The hunger, the plagues, the suicides. The greed, the lies, the tyrannies. The rising seas that drown our farmlands. The hordes from the burning south that would invade us, that could put guns in our hands despite our gun-free oaths.

Silent thoughts, spoken thoughts.

Our families, our friends, our few neighbors. Most of us seeking answers, answers to an ever more dangerous, disturbed, unreliable world. Autocracies, oligarchies, democracies abandoned, failing institutions. Fascist patterns in country after country. And most alarmingly, as the reality of global warming takes hold, the rapidly growing unrest, the massive crowd responses—enraged violence, the mass movement north of peoples seeking survival, escape from growing horrors. Droughts, food production dropping, devastating heat waves, violent weather, floods, rising seas. Governments hopeless.

Do I dream?

Were we aware, Ramiro, you and I, even as we founded Twinflower Farm, were we aware of its strategic value? Did we foresee barricading ourselves against the migrations, the marauders that find our island? And did we expect to be living still in this doom we obsessed on so?

Isolated, an island, though reachable from the mainland by boat—even a ferry back then. High rainfall, northern temperate, fertile, potentially self-sustainable, sparse human population, much wild life.

This, our home. Once the homesteader's cabin, transformed over the years. One room, that's it.

At one end, a mattress, piles of pillows, cushions, blankets, rugs. A wardrobe, clothes hooks on the log walls, sagging shelves, books. A wood stove on the back wall, this table, two rickety chairs, a bench, a sofa, more rugs and pillows. Two of my sketches of our little Ceci. Photos. The bathroom at the other end behind an unused curtain. An ancient tub on lion's legs, a composting toilet, a sink, its enamel badly chipped.

Years ago we'd added a small mud room. Through the wall between the two windows opposite the stove. Under its own little roof, our only door. Two closets, shelves, hooks.

On the lintel, above the door, is your Luger in its halter, a shimmer of light from our lantern on the leather hoster, just polished yesterday. And beside it is my wee ballerina twirling on her silver toes, your thirty-third birthday, Vermejo College.

A clap, sharp, loud, nearby. A shriek! Running feet, curses. JR's voice, Damn, what the fuck! It's me, JR. My great grandson Wally? Help! They got me, my thigh. We stumble out of bed. I grab my Luger off the lintel, unbar the door. Lakeside in the moonlight, lying on the bank, is a figure in white, and another, dark, kneeling over her.

More shots. Rapid fire. Against a sky of northern lights, a line of figures on the clifftop over the cave. Wally, he waves us back. We drop behind our wood pile. I peer out. My Luger, it's firing, vicious jolts, futile shots? But from cabins near the cliff assault weapons are blazing. Two figures from clifftop drop into darkness.

The others disappear.

Wally in JR's place, low voices, hand signals to stand guard, half-circling the cabins that back onto the cliff. Two bodies on the talus, a woman, a teenage boy.

Omar and Wally carry JR to our cabin, lay her on our table. Omar, an ER nurse for several years back east, Wally, still trembling, holds the flashlight. A clean shot right through the thigh, bone seems sound, bleeding controlled with pressure, prognosis positive. Maybe stitch it up tomorrow. Our hoard of boiled bandages reused yet again.

What happened to our no-guns rule? What happened to us, to Lori and me? Must I accept that my life may be by way of another's death?

Cool equinox, Lori and I headed south. Yes, south. Burlap bags, walking sticks. Bedraggled, weary. Pot pipes still warming our nights.

Cold sweat, waiting at the north end of a bridge for a surge of hundreds headed north. North for the promised land. Loaded carts, bicycles, guns. A hay wagon pulled by two emaciated horses, carrying dozens, stops in front of us, turns around, unloads at gunpoint. Screams, two shot, bodies pushed over the railing into the river.

Yes south, many weeks still to our mountain home, to Los Etchos. No trains, no buses. Will someone stop for us, will anyone be heading into the burning south, fifteen hundred miles? Perhaps truckers returning to the Mexican border? Professional coyotes ferrying the monied few from among the desperate legions, trucking them ever north, claiming a secret border crossing to some Shangri-La in the Canadian wilderness. A blighted and wild-fired wilderness rapidly filling with rival hungry communities.

Yes. To the Sierra Madre Occidental. High in cool mountains, forests, meadows. Our Mango Tree.

Dust, a crushing sun, the rank burro sweat. Two days from forested mountains to the sea, stiff-legged Manolo and me. A burlap sack thumping against his haunch. Lumps of chickpea cheese, crusts of twice-baked mango-flour bread. Lori slipped in slices of dried mango sprinkled with marijuana powder. An ancient pocket knife, a gourd replenished with stale water from an arroyo seepage, a battered aluminum bowl. Tied to the pommel in a cloth pouch, my holstered Luger, a box of ammunition. Both of us saddle-sore, exhausted, creaking with age.

The sea lies before us, reaching out toward the afternoon sun, thirty, forty minutes above the horizon. A glittering path on a calm white surface, a vast bay protected from the open Sea of Cortez by a far-off line of mangrove islands. A chug-chugging, a black dot creeps across the sun's path. A lone bottom trawl, maybe the last of the hopeless, scraping up whatever may be left of life, ready to risk the cesium, the mercury, the early death.

Painfully, I swing a leg over Manolo's rump and slide off into the dune grass. As a signal to graze, I drop the hackamore ropes, mecate of horsehair I braided maybe ninety years ago sitting under old Rag Bag's Mango Tree. Manolo, my grumpy old friend, he looks back at me, brays half-heartedly, noses the grasses, pisses fitfully.

The sea stirs with the wake of the trawler. The tide is in, high into the dunes, nibbling deeper into the land. A clump of sand-verbena floats loose, its purple flower tipping into the sea. A tamarisk teeters, its roots exposed. The mesquite and the ocotillo will be next. An organpipe-etcho's blackened skeleton lies half submerged, another still stands, ten–twelve feet out in the quiet sea, its lattice of bones against the bleeding sun. The skies are empty, no gulls, no plunging pelicans, no curlews to chase wavelets in the dwindling strip of sand. A lone heron wades in the eel grass, patient, searching for a last morsel.

The rising sea, the dying sea. I touch the silver iguanita spoon hanging by my heart.

I untie the burlap sack, drink a mouthful of fetid water from the gourd. Manolo slurps up the rest from his bowl. I take the cloth bag from the saddle, pocket the knife, pickup the bag of my holstered Luger. On the leather flap is the imprinted swastika surrounded by Kriegsmarine Ubootwaffe. I take the ammunition magazine from its pocket on the holster, put the holster down on a bit of withered kelp in the dune grass. I rub the magazine in my hands, the baseball pitcher's rite. Now, left foot up on a clod of grass, right foot back, turned out. Hands together, in front of my face. Quick glance back at first base over the left shoulder, smooth into the windup, the pitch.

The Luger's next.

Two burials, an intractable sea.

I keep the holster.

And would that Mamá were here with her lotion for my pitcher's shoulder.

I am back, exhausted, bones, joints moaning. Hair scraggly, or...look again, is it shining black? My young me, my young Lori, gone? A dream, a Luger, a waking, when, to what?

Our hammocks are slung side by side from low branches of Mango Tree. On the brick tiles between us, one tile with the hoof print of a deer, is a bowl of mangoes. Sitting up, I take one, hold it in my hands, turning it, rubbing it gently, seeking purchase for a three-fingers pitch.

With my pocket knife I slice into the rose-ripe glow of the fruit. Sweet, resinous, I lick drops from the back of my hand. Here, a slice of mango, Lori sweet. I touch her cheek. So velvet smooth. Her parted lips.

I swing my legs out of the hammock, reach for Ceci's swing rope. Sweet Ceci, laughing as she spins. I join her, we swing, we dance. Lori climbs out of her hammock, with her harmonica she picks up our rhythm. Boogie Woogie from our shipyard wartime days. Yesterday, so many years ago? Ceci, she runs out, gives a slice of mango to a neighbor's mut, laughs, skips to loud ranchera, a radio in a cart that's bumping by.

I put the mango pit at the end of a line of them drying in the sun, pick two dry ones, carry them to Rag Bag's mortar waiting for us on her bench of adobe bricks. My knife, Rag Bag's pestle. A river stone to fit her hand. I straddle the bench, begin the cutting, pounding, grinding. Mango flour for tonight's tortillas. Some extras to the needful of those who stay on in our village . . . to the end.

A white-wing dove murmurs high in the secrets of Mango Tree.

Dim against the evening sky, the foglia of a branch forms a leaf-green gown, a smiling face, a crown of golden fruit.

I hold my shining silver Iguanito to my heart.

Manolo mutters in his pen behind Mango Tree.

Children's happy voices in the distance.

A rooster calls, an accordion answers.

The voices of Los Etchos.

Home.

**ROBERT CABOT** is the author of *The Joshua Tree*, *That Sweetest Wine*, *The Isle of Kheria*, and *Time's Up! A Memoir of the American Century*. He is a veteran of many campaigns of World War II in North Africa and Europe. He received degrees from Harvard College and Yale Law School, served for ten years in the Marshall Plan and foreign aid programs in Italy, Thailand, Sri Lanka, and Washington, D.C., and resigned from the foreign service in protest over U.S. policy in Southeast Asia. He has since worked with intentional communities, the citizen diplomacy movement, and environmental and social change projects. He lived for many years in Italy and Greece, returning to the U.S. in a solo transatlantic sail with his thirty-foot sloop in 1976.

Writing, however, is his first love. Now, at 99, he has written *The Mango Tree*. Cabot is a fellow of the National Endowment for the Arts, the McDowell Colony, the Virginia Center for the Creative Arts, and the Ucross Foundation.

Cabot lives on Whidbey Island, Washington, as well as in a mountain town in southeastern Arizona with his wife Penny. Between them they have six children and many grandchildren.

www.ingramcontent.com/pod-product-compliance
Lightning Source LLC
Chambersburg PA
CBHW060538310726
48982CB00009B/1304/J

* 9 7 9 8 9 8 8 6 8 0 3 0 7 *